HENHOUSE HIGH JINX

MR. STEVENS AND FRIENDS

BY

ROB DAVIES

ILLUSTRATED BY

ERIC COMEAU

Order this book online at www.trafford.com
or email orders@trafford.com

Most Trafford titles are also available at major online book retailers.

Printed in the United States of America.

ISBN: 978-1-4669-9491-1 (sc)
ISBN: 978-1-4669-9492-8 (hc)

Library of Congress Control Number: 2013909373

Trafford rev. 11/26/2013

 www.trafford.com

North America & international
toll-free: 1 888 232 4444 (USA & Canada)
fax: 812 355 4082

Mr. Stevens dedicates this story to Jordan Stephens:

A young man who takes all the challenges life throws at him with a positive attitude and a smile on his face!

What doesn't break you will only make you stronger!

Meet the Cast and
Crew of Mr. Stevens
and Friends.

Dirk Stevens AKA Mr. Stevens

Mr. Stevens is the official leader of Farmer Johnston's Coop. Dirk became a barnyard icon after risking his life to save all the chickens in the yard from a painful demise at the hands of King Jack's Buffet House. You can read all about Dirk's heroics in *Trouble in the Coop*.

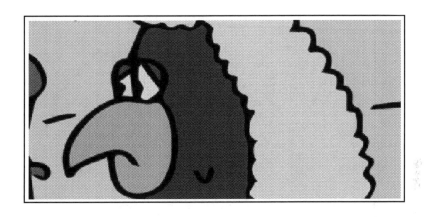

Derek Stevens

Derek Stevens is Dirk's older brother. After spending most of his life teasing and tormenting his younger sibling, the tide has turned and he now lives in the shadow of his iconic brother. Resentful, and full of spite, Derek spends every waking moment hoping his brother will fail.

Sandra Thompson

The ravishing young pullet who Dirk has fallen comb over wattles in love with. Daughter of the former leader, Mr. Thompson, Sandra is a kind and sensitive hen who believes that Dirk is the key to success in the coop.

Darryl Earley (Head) and
Dwayne Davies (Fist)

Two roosters with the combined intelligence quotient of a dead sea anemone. Best friends, mindless followers, and unmistakable morons, they are never far from their slightly more astute best bud Derek Stevens.

Rick Comeau

Toughest looking cockerel to ever settle in Farmer Johnston's coop. An import from Farmer Beaton's barn, Rick has differing views on both life and responsibility. Hens love him, roosters want to be him, and his arrival has thrown the barnyard into mass chaos!

External Anatomy
of a Chicken

Glossary of Land Fowl Terms

Bestie: Best friend. A very good amigo.

BFF: "Best Fowl Forever" – An expression used to express ultimate friendship between two chickens.

Cockerel: Young male chicken.

Cockle-Doodle-Doo-Tube: A place where videos are posted publicly for all chickens to enjoy.

Face-Beak: Popular social networking site for chickens.

Fowl: Birds, like a chicken, that are generally tasty when deep-fried and served with dipping sauce.

Hen: Female chicken.

High Jinx Meter: Measures the amount of hen drama present in the henhouse.

Mother-Cluck: Almighty fowl of worship.

Pullet: Young female chicken.

Rooster Club: Male version of the henhouse. A place for roosters to kick back and do guy stuff.

WTF: "What The Fowl" – An expression commonly used when a chicken is experiencing modest confusion.

One

A faint ray of sunlight peeped over the horizon, illuminating Farmer Johnston's chicken coop. As the inside of the henhouse brightened, the ladies began to stir. A big day lay ahead of them, the last one before Farmer Johnston collected the eggs to take to market. Their job was to ensure the nests were stuffed to the brim. Gladys slowly rose and stretched out her wings.

As had become the custom of most of the hens in the house, Gladys began the day by checking out the news on Face-Beak. Face-Beak was the latest in land fowl social media. It gave the chickens the ability to send messages and pictures, share important information, and gossip with one another. This could be done by posting messages privately in individual nests or publicly on stall walls. Gladys smiled as she saw the post her best friend Janet had put up on her stall wall: A picture of the two of them playing Kanasta together. Underneath she had scrawled the letters BFF and surrounded them with a big red heart. *Janet is the best friend a hen could ever have*, Gladys thought to herself, her heart filled with joy.

Dawn continued to break as Mr. Stevens slowly roused himself and waddled out to his newly acquired perch on the fencepost. It was show time and he was the main attraction. Throwing a wing in the air like a seasoned rock star, he bellowed out a shrill, "Cockle-Doodle-Doo!" The sun was coming up and another busy day was upon them. The barnyard animals began to rise from their peaceful slumbers ready to tackle the arduous tasks ahead. Mr. Stevens stood on the perch enjoying the moment to its fullest. It was his third day of wake-up call duty, and he was loving every minute of it.

Not every rooster shared in his newfound joy. Mr. Stevens' older brother Derek, was *not* loving every minute of it. Truth be told, he was jealous and downright resentful of his brother's newfound fame. The two had never seen eye to eye, and ever since Dirk Stevens had heroically saved the coop from an evil buffet titan, the animosity level had risen to an all-new high. As a result, Derek jumped at every chance to knock his younger sibling down a peg or two. Sensing a golden opportunity, he decided to pounce.

"Nice wake-up call," he cackled at Mr. Stevens. "Really well done."

"Thanks Derek," Mr. Stevens replied, oblivious to the sarcasm in his brother's voice. "I think I was a little high pitched, but I'm working on it."

"A *little* High pitched?" Derek scoffed. "I should say it was. By the screech you let out I figured someone was squeezing your wattles." Derek laughed as he cracked open a bag of salt 'n' vinegar chips, and smirked rudely at his brother. "Sounded like the farmer jabbed you with a pitchfork or something."

Mr. Stevens opened his beak to respond, but then thought better of it. On top of being a chip-devouring ignoramus, Derek was also a petty and bitter bird. Engaging in a war of words was exactly what he wanted. Responding would start off yet another riff between the two. Mr. Stevens chose the high road and ignored Derek's comments. Besides, it was almost time for the morning feed, and he didn't want to be late. There was nothing quite like a dose of fresh mealworm to get the day started off right.

All the coop's chickens assembled at the food trough, drooling at the beak in anticipation of the day's first meal. As Farmer Johnston marched across the yard, they were surprised to see he wasn't carrying the usual sack of grub. Rather, he carried a rough and tumble looking rooster under his arm. Gently, he set him down on the ground.

"Everyone," the farmer announced. "This is Rick. He has come to us from Farmer Beaton's up the road. Please give him a warm welcome while I go finish preparing your breakfast." The farmer smiled down reassuringly at Rick, who returned his look with an icy glare.

The entire coop stood and gawked. Rick was unlike anything they had ever seen before. There was a menacing look to him that the roosters found quite intimidating. Although somewhat frightened, they all envied his tough appearance. Rick's presence, was having the opposite effect on the hens. They all stared at him in star-struck awe, captivated by his bad-boy image. It could have been the tattoos that covered his wings, the piercing through his comb or the fact that he wore a studded leather vest. Whatever the reason, Rick's sudden arrival had caused quite a buzz in the barnyard.

Mr. Stevens was the first to approach the farm's newest resident. "Welcome to the coop," he said warmly, extending a wing. "I'm Mr. Stevens."

Rick stared at the coop leader like he'd just had a bowel movement in his nest. "Get preened you tool!" he snarled, rudely pushing his way past Mr. Stevens and heading towards the Rooster Club. "Come get me for lunch," he demanded without even turning around. "You idiots have tired me out already. I need a nap."

The whole brood stood in shock. Rick had just scornfully pushed by their leader without batting an eyelash. No rooster had ever done anything so brash and brazen before. Mr. Stevens was too stunned to even be upset. "He must be feeling a little uneasy in his new surroundings," he announced, a slight trace of embarrassment evident in his voice. "Let's give him some time to settle in."

The chickens stood and stared at Mr. Stevens for an extra moment before carrying on with their daily business. Derek, who had watched the entire episode, stood giggling by the food trough. When the others were out of earshot the chirping began. "Nice job pal. Three days in and your authority is already being usurped. By a dude who has only lived here for two minutes, I should add. Stuff like this never happened when Mr. Thompson was in command."

Mr. Stevens, normally very adept at controlling his temper when it came to his vindictive brother, suddenly exploded. There were certain touchy subjects, and the comparison his gluttonous brother had just made was one of them. "Have another chip you voracious imbecile!" he exclaimed angrily. "I hope you choke on the next one!" Turning in a huff, he stormed off to give his rattled nerves a chance to settle.

Derek grinned as Mr. Stevens stomped across the yard. He, like a bothersome tick, had finally gotten under his brother's skin.

Two

There were a few less fowl present when Farmer Johnston returned with his well-rounded breakfast of mealworm and corn niblets. Most of the hens had bolted back to the henhouse immediately following Rick's introduction. Extra calories were the last thing the young ladies needed if they wanted to capture his attention. Or so they at least believed. It would certainly take a little extra fluffing and preening to successfully seduce the coop's newest beau.

The roosters took advantage of the hens' absence and stuffed their beaks with the delicious eats. Chomping down on the fresh kibble, they talked non-stop of the rebellious young ruffian that had just taken the barnyard by storm. "Did you see those gnarly tattoos?" Darryl asked his good buddy Dwayne.

"Sure did bird," Dwayne replied. "Dude is sporting some serious ink. I like the one of the skull and cross wings."

"Me too!" Darryl remarked, bobbing his head back and forth. "I wish I had the wattles to get tattooed like that."

"Agreed," Dwayne concurred. "Imagine how tough that would look. The hens would be all over us for sure!"

Both friends stood, chomping their meals, when a sudden thought struck Darryl. "We should go get him for the feed," he suggested. "That'd put us in his good books right off the bat. Maybe he'd even be kind enough to give us a few tips on how to be awesome."

Dwayne nodded in agreement before suddenly being struck with a brainwave of his own. "I have an even better idea," he replied with a grin. "Let's take him his food personally. There's nothing like a little breakfast in the nest to get on a fella's good side. He'd totally think we were 'the giblets' if we did that."

Darryl jiggled his head and chirped his support of the plan. The two quickly scrounged up some mealworm to take to their new hero.

*   *   *

In the henhouse, a surge of energy was bubbling through the female population. The hens had all settled back in their stalls for some frantic self-beautification. Rick could walk by at any moment thus they needed to look their very best. First impressions meant everything when it came to chicken attraction. Make-up was slopped on by the gallon as each young lass tried to outdo the next in a quest to capture Rick's love and affection.

"No way could I eat breakfast today," Gladys piped up. "Can't afford to let a few extra calories ruin my chances with Rick."

"Totally," Janet replied. "I think I'm going to go for a little run around the pig pen before I settle down for the day to lay my eggs. Hopefully shed a few ounces in case he saunters by."

"Oh Janet, you look great already," Gladys called out to her BFF. "Say, be honest, do these saddle feathers make my rump look fat? I oiled them up so they don't stick out as much, but I can't tell."

Janet took a quick peek at Gladys' huge rump. "No," she lied. "Not at all. That extra grease has had a real thinning effect on your back end. You look like a million bucks. Irresistible!" As Gladys smiled at her friend's praise, similar dialogue was running rampant throughout the henhouse. Every hen wanted to make sure she looked hot and sexy to impress Rick.

Well, maybe not *every* hen. Sandra Thompson stood back and watched the foolishness, shaking her head in disgust. As the ladies complimented each other, she was well aware of the underlying aura of deceit weaving itself through the various conversations.

I wonder if these gals have considered the fact that they are prepping themselves to attract the same rooster? she asked herself doubtfully. *If this turns into a competition, things could get very messy.*

Sandra stared up at the 'High Jinx Alert Meter' that sat above the door leading out to the yard. There were five distinct colours that carefully measured the level of hen drama in the henhouse.

<u>Green</u> meant all was wonderful.

<u>Blue</u> indicated that slight tensions were present.

<u>Yellow</u> gave notice of a growing negative energy.

Orange signified a major issue had developed and a serious crisis was looming.

Red represented full-scale Henhouse High Jinx. A meltdown was unavoidable.

The needle was slowly shifting from green to blue. Although safe for the moment, Sandra was deeply concerned that a competition for Rick would have a negative impact on the brood. She had seen hen drama escalate before, and the chaotic results were never pretty. Sandra vowed to watch the meter closely and report to Mr. Stevens immediately if things appeared to be spiraling out of control.

* * *

Darryl and Dwayne arrived at the Rooster Club and carefully approached Rick, who was relaxing in his stall. Drawing closer, they noticed rings of smoke passing above him. "Is he smoking?" Darryl asked Dwayne curiously. He had never seen a rooster smoke before. For that matter, he had never seen a cigarette before either.

"I think he is," replied Dwayne nervously. They had always been taught as young cockerels that smoking was a very nasty and unhealthy habit to take up. As a result, Farmer Johnston's coop was of the non-smoking variety. Tobacco of any kind was strictly taboo.

"Uh, Mr. Rick, sir, we brought you some food," Darryl stammered, breaking the ice. "Where would you like us to leave it?"

Rick slowly turned around, cigarette hanging from his beak. "You boys are bothering my 'lone-time'," he barked. "Just leave it on the floor there. I'll get to it when I get to it."

The not so dynamic duo stood and stared at Rick with admiration. His voice was awesome, so gravely and tough. His movements were awesome, the way he shrugged them off like they were tiny mounds of sheep dung. Rick, and everything about him, was awesome.

"Did you guys hear me?" Rick snarled. "I said, leave the food over there. What are you, stupid or something? Do I need to talk slower or spell it out for you?"

Darryl and Dwayne shook their heads and carefully placed the food tray on the floor of Rick's stall. Both looked back at him hopefully before Darryl finally mustered up enough courage to speak. "Listen Rick," he said uneasily. "You may not have noticed the signs, but this is a non-smoking coop."

"Really dumb rule," Dwayne quickly added before Rick could respond. "I hate it."

"Totally dumb," Darryl agreed. "But, uh, I'd hate for a cool bird like you to land in any hot water because of some ridiculous regulation."

Rick glared at the two simpletons and took another haul off his cigarette; blowing a waft of foul smelling, second hand smoke back in their faces. "I saw the signs just fine," he retorted with a sly grin. "All six of them. How could I not see them? Blasted things are posted everywhere. *However,* I chose to ignore them," he snarled. "I tend to ignore a lot of things that I think are stupid. It's amazing I haven't chosen to ignore you two idiots yet."

Darryl and Dwayne stood silently; sporting their trademark, blank gazes. The two were definitely not the sharpest roosters in Farmer Johnston's barnyard. Combined, they sported an IQ roughly equivalent to that of a dead skunk. They weren't really sure how to respond, so they just tilted their heads, opened their beaks, and stared at Rick.

Rick stared back. Finally realizing he wasn't dealing with the intellectually gifted, his tone lightened a little. "Listen fellas, you two seem like you have the potential to not be lame," he finally remarked. "And, you did bring me food. So here, I have a little something for you." Rick reached under his wing, pulled out a couple of cigarettes and held them out for the boys to examine. "Have a smoke boys," he offered. "It'll help you digest your mealworm, and make you a lot less gassy."

Dwayne looked at Darryl, Darryl looked at Dwayne, and Dwayne slowly nodded. "Sure man that would be great. It's been awhile since I was able to enjoy a good smoke," he lied. Truth was, like Darryl, Dwayne had never seen a real cigarette either. But, in fear of looking like a loser in front of Rick, he extended his wing and graciously accepted the freshly lit gift. He wasn't really sure what to do with it so he stuck it in his beak and sucked in deeply.

Dwayne realized, almost instantly, that smoking wasn't his cup of tea. As he drew in the foul tasting poisons, his lungs began palpitating, doing their best to reject the toxic sludge. Dwayne's face reddened and his cheeks bloated out like a puffer fish. Eyes bulging, his comb involuntarily shillyshallied back and forth spastically. With a loud sputter the cigarette shot out of his beak like a cannonball and landed at Rick's feet. Dwayne keeled over, hacking up a stream of yellowy mucus; his body trying to rid itself of the grimy tar that had just infiltrated his bronchial tubes.

Rick chuckled as he picked up the glowing cigarette with his wing. "Guess it must have been a *real* long while since your last smoke," he scoffed. "Like maybe never?" Dwayne was too busy wheezing and coughing to disagree. Shaking his head in disgust, Rick turned his attention to Darryl.

"How about you, rubberneck? You any more suave than this moron?"

Darryl responded with a vigorous nod. "Uh, well, ya, for sure," he chirped. "I smoke all the time. Can't get more suave than me."

"Sure," Rick replied sarcastically. "We'll see about that."

Darryl's smoking experience turned out even worse than Dwayne's. As he inhaled, a burning sensation festered in his lungs. The taste in his beak could be likened to that of cleaning a public toilet with his tongue. Collapsing to the ground, he choked and sputtered, as his body tried to stop the convulsions in his trachea and nasal passage.

Rick leaned over, reclaimed the glowing stick from Darryl, and stuck it back in his own beak. "Here I thought you guys could be cool. You're nothing more than a couple of losers. Get your sorry combs out of my stall! Beat it!"

Both Darryl and Dwayne tried to pull themselves together, still gasping and gagging. Both dropped their heads in shame. They really were a couple of idiots. Fools. There was no way they would ever be cool enough to hang out with Rick. He was way too awesome for them.

As they turned to leave Rick put out his wing, stopping them in their tracks. A thought had struck him. "Hey, before you idiots take off, I might have an idea that could help you guys save some face," he offered, before pretending to reconsider. "Nah, forget it. I doubt you two chumps are up to the challenge."

Darryl and Dwayne shared an optimistic glance with one another. "Oh we definitely are," Darryl chirped, sensing a glimmer of hope.

"Absolutely!" Dwayne agreed. "We're always having to save face. What do you need us to do?"

Rick paused momentarily, to build the suspense. "Well, it's kind of a risky venture, if you know what I mean," he replied. "I'm not sure you two clowns would be able to handle it. You gotta be really tough. A lot tougher than what you just demonstrated."

"Oh, Rick man, we can handle it." Darryl exclaimed. "One time we played chicken with Farmer Johnston's combine harvester. If we can handle that, we can handle anything."

"Ya right!" Rick muttered sarcastically. "I saw some real evidence of that just a minute ago, Smokey."

"Seriously Rick, we were just out of practice. That little display was a fluke. We're way cooler than that! We can do whatever it is you need us to do," Dwayne pleaded. "Let us save face, please!"

Rick looked at both Dwayne and Darryl and shrugged. *What the heck*, he thought to himself handing each of the boys another cigarette. "I'm gonna give you both a chance to try this again. But, before I do, there's something I need to know. Have you two meatheads ever heard of something called Cockle-Doodle-Doo-Tube?"

Three

Back at the henhouse, the ladies were so engaged in self-beautification they forgot all about laying their high quality Omega-3 eggs. Instead of building up Farmer Johnston's stockpile, they were busy building up their own make-up foundations. All were seeking to gain the edge in the competition for Rick as they put the finishing touches on their eye shadow and mascara.

"I'm sure he was eying me this morning," Gladys announced proudly to Janet for the eight hundredth time. "When he first arrived I saw him turn his head and his eyes glanced over me; over *all* of me. I totally see a little of he and I rubbing beaks at the water trough in the very near future."

Janet glared back at her friend in disgust. She was tired of listening to Gladys ramble on and on about how she was going to land Rick. She'd spent the entire morning blabbing to any hens that would listen, trying to convince them that Rick was totally into her. Most of the girls had already tuned her out, so Janet bore the brunt of the boasting. Even though Gladys was her best friend there was no denying that she was about as attractive as a rotting skunk. Enough was enough.

Finally reaching her tipping point, Janet lashed out. Friend or not, she had had enough of Gladys' constant yapping. "The only way Rick will be rubbing beaks with you is if the rest of us drop dead and then he tragically loses his vision," she blurted out nastily. "That chubby saddle of yours is going to do nothing more than make him want to throw up his mealworm."

Gladys stopped fluffing her keel and looked over at her friend with both shock and despair. "What? You told me the greased feathers had a slimming look," she replied, her voice full of hurt. "I asked you. You said I looked great."

"Great if you're trying to look like a balloon," Janet snorted back. "You should try cutting back on all the extra cornmeal you've been chowing down on lately. You're like a vacuum out there during feeding time, sucking back all the niblets before the rest of us have time to even open our beaks."

Gladys stood and stared, amazed at the words coming out of her best friend's beak. Even though BFFs were prone to the odd argument, Janet's words had struck a nerve. Deciding that two could play the insult game, Gladys decided to take a few shots of her own.

"Well Janet, I'd rather have on a few extra pounds than look like someone slapped me in the head with a bag of spare ski-doo parts," she steamed. "I can diet. You will always look like an elephant just stomped on your face."

The henhouse suddenly grew very, very, quiet. The other hens all perked up and began to listen more intently to the bickering. A battle between besties didn't happen everyday and no hen wanted to miss it. They took great enjoyment listening to Gladys and Janet hurling inappropriate insults back and forth.

Sandra Thompson, who was good friends with both, could not believe her ears. Two best friends, fighting over a rooster they had only seen for a split second. *What were they thinking?* It was when Janet poked fun of Gladys' gas issues that Sandra decided to step in and mediate.

"Listen girls. Both of you need to calm down. There's no use getting worked up over some rooster you don't even know. You two have been friends forever and nothing should ever interfere with that bond. Especially some leather-clad cretin from another barnyard."

Gladys wheeled around angrily and glared at Sandra, "Shut your beak, and mind your own business. This is between me and crater-face. It has nothing to do with you, you prude."

Sandra stood in shock, taken aback by her friend's rude outburst. Before she could respond, mayhem broke out.

"It's him, it's him!" a young pullet squawked, pointing with her wing out into the yard. "It's Rick. He's heading to the water trough!"

It took a split second as realization kicked in before the hens charged for the yard like a stampede of starving lions chasing a wounded gazelle. At top speed, the ladies pushed, shoved, clawed, scratched and bit their way by one another. Sandra ducked into her stall to avoid being trampled as the crowd pressed through. A quick glance at the High Jinx Meter told her all she needed to know. Tension was beginning to escalate. The meter now wavered between blue and yellow; an alarmingly quick increase to the drama level for one morning. The henhouse, it seemed, was heading down a slippery and dangerous slope. One that could potentially have disastrous results. Unfortunately, for the moment, Sandra Thompson seemed to be the only hen concerned.

Rick stood by the water trough leaning against a loose board on the fence. He stuck out his keel and flexed his wings, showing off his numerous tattoos. As the hens came into view, he lit up another cigarette, tilted his head back, and started blowing smoke rings in the air.

"He is such a dream," one hen commented, her voice filled with lust.

"Such a rebel," added another. "Look at those muscular wings, and keel! I would give my right wattle to preen his saddle."

The hens stood, admiring from a distance as Rick continued being awesome, smoking and staring at the sky. Finally, after what seemed like forever and a day, Gladys mustered up the nerve to leave the safety of the group and approach. All the other hens whispered excitedly to each other. First contact was about to be made.

Waddling up to the trough with an extra wiggle and bounce to her step she cheerfully introduced herself. "Hey Rick," she said in her deepest, sexiest voice, "I'm Gladys."

"Good for you." Rick replied coolly, blowing another smoke ring in the air. Slowly he turned his head and sized Gladys up. "Hey yourself."

"I want to welcome you to our coop," she continued, taking post directly beside him. "How do you like it so far?"

Rick looked at her with a gaze of indifference. "This coop sucks," he replied. After a moment's pause, and a couple more puffs he added, "But that's about to change."

"Is that because *I'm* here now?" she asked expectantly, her voice cracking as she stared into his steely grey eyes.

Rick glowered back at her and smirked. "Uh, no. It's because *I'm* here now. I plan on turning this place into something way more exciting. This eternal boredom is giving me pains in my gullet."

"Oooh. That will be amazing," Gladys replied, brushing her wing against Rick's keel. "I love a rooster who isn't afraid to make a change."

Rick looked at her and shook his head. "Good for you," he shot back in annoyance, spurning her advance. "Is there a point to this conversation or are you purposely standing in my sunlight?" He motioned to the large shadow that Gladys was casting.

Embarrassed, Gladys awkwardly shifted to the left, moving her silhouette off the irritated rooster. "Oh, I am so sorry Rick," she apologized. "I didn't notice."

"Whatever," he snorted, turning his back to her. "I need to get back to sunning myself."

Gladys stood and waited for an awkward moment before turning and shuffling back to the brood. All the hens quickly crowded around to hear her tale. What had he said? What had they talked about? Gladys was only too happy to be the center of attention. Janet stood to the side, jealousy bubbling in her veins.

"He is such a dream. I totally think he's into me. Totally!" Gladys bragged.

"If he's so into you, why are you back here with us then?" Janet retorted, her words laced with envy. "Why aren't the two of you off rubbing beaks behind the barn?"

Gladys chose to ignore her friend's bitterness. "Rick says he is going to make this coop way more exciting. I, for one, can hardly wait. This place really does need a facelift." Speaking a mile a minute Gladys narrated her adventure with Rick. The hens clung to every word she said. Excitement filled the air. First contact had been made and they wanted to hear every juicy detail.

"We'll see who he really likes." Janet mumbled as she turned in a huff and headed back to the henhouse. Something had to be done about Gladys. Her brazen behaviour could not be ignored. She had just thrown herself at Rick without thinking about any of the other hens. Punishment was definitely needed for such self-centered actions.

An ingenious idea suddenly hatched in Janet's little brain. She knew exactly how Gladys would pay for her selfishness. And she would pay dearly. Her visions of attracting Rick would soon be pipe dreams. In fact, good old Gladys might never attract another rooster again. Her illusions of a life with the coop's new rebel were about to quickly fade away.

Four

"Hey guys, what are you up to?" Derek asked his two best friends as the three congregated together near the water trough. They hadn't seen each other all morning and Derek was anxious to catch up. Both Dwayne and Darryl looked at each other and shrugged.

"Not much," Darryl replied. "We just came back from having a smoke with Rick."

"A smoke?" Derek sputtered. "Since when did you two clowns start smoking?"

"Since this morning," Dwayne piped up. "Cigarettes are awesome!" he lied.

Derek shook his head in disgust. "You two fools are going to end up in trouble. This is a non-smoking coop. You know that. There are signs everywhere."

Darryl stuck out his keel and stared at Derek. "Ya, well, things are changing around here. It's time we took a stand against some of these stupid rules."

Derek looked back at his friend, dumbfounded. "What do you mean stupid? We live in a chicken coop that is full of hay, and made of wood. One little spark and it's the Hindenburg all over again."

"Derek, don't be such a wiener," Darryl remarked rudely. "It's no big deal. Relax and live a little. You can come with us next time and see what you've been missing."

"A little is all you idiots are gonna live if you keep smoking in the coop!" Derek replied indignantly. "What do you mean, no big deal? I can't believe you two would do something so moronic. Not only is this a huge breach of safety for all of us but think of your own health. Smoking isn't exactly a life extending habit."

"Health, shmealth," Dwayne chirped. "Since when did you become a doctor? Stop your prissy whining or Rick won't want anything to do with you."

"I'm not sure that's such a bad thing Dwayne. Prissy whining? Health-Shmealth? Listen to yourself. I know you're not exactly a Mensa member, but do you really believe the stupid things you're saying? Rick has you brainwashed." Derek replied with ire in his voice. "Do you really believe that it's cool to sit around smoking all day?"

Dwayne nodded. "Of course I believe it. I believe it because it's true. You only live once Derek, and I'm tired of my daily schedule consisting of twelve glorious hours doing absolutely nothing! I need some excitement. I need some fun! Rick provides both. He hasn't brainwashed either one of us, you chip-chomping buffoon. Rather, he has shown us the light."

"Yeah," Darryl agreed. "For example, just this morning, he taught us how to smoke *properly*. At first we coughed and wheezed and looked a little silly, but now we're like chimneys."

Dwayne quickly jumped in, "He showed us that underneath all the uneaten kibble and little piles of chicken dung, there is a hotbed of excitement waiting to blossom, right here in our coop. Rick is a visionary, and definitely the best thing to happen to this barnyard in a long, long time. Come along *with* us Derek. Hang out with Rick. You'll love him. Have a smoke, take the edge off, and see what it's like to be awesome."

Derek shook his head in wonder. "I enjoy *not* being awesome, thank you very much. I'm quite content to sit here and eat my chips while you cluck-heads puff your lives away," he squawked angrily. "I never thought my two best friends could be lured into acting so brainlessly."

Dwayne scoffed at his friend's words. "And we never thought that our best friend could be such a dud," he fired back. "C'mon Darryl, let's go see our new bestie, Rick. He won't squash our fun."

"Yeah! I could use another smoke anyway," Darryl agreed. "There's way too much fresh air in my lungs."

Just before they waddled off, Dwayne turned to Derek, "Rick has us doing some cool stuff for Cockle-Doodle-Doo-Tube later on this afternoon. Maybe if you change your mind and aren't feeling so lame, you'll think about joining up with us at the Rooster Club."

"What in the world is Cockle-Doodle-Doo-Tube?" Derek asked in wonder.

Darryl cracked a smile. "It is awesome. Just like Rick. Basically it is this thing we can hook into our T.V. that allows us to view movies and shows that we make ourselves."

"Not only that," Dwayne added. "Other barns that have it can tune in to our shows as well."

Derek threw his wings in the air and let out an exasperated groan. "What stuff could you two possibly be doing for Cockle-Doodle-Doo-Tube?" he asked, frustration evident in his tone.

"Apparently we're going to be the main features in a new video Rick is making. Me and Dwayne are going to be famous," Darryl bragged.

"Of all the roosters on the farm, why in the name of Mother-Cluck would he choose you two meat-birds to be his stars?" Derek queried, shaking his head.

"Obviously he recognizes good talent when he sees it," Darryl remarked with an air of pride. "It's like a sixth sense for someone as awesome as Rick. Just remember, you heard it here first. Dwayne and I are going to be stars."

More like meteors, Derek thought to himself. *Big, dumb chunks of rock hurtling through space with no direction.*

As the moronic duo made off to find Rick, Derek stood befuddled and alone, left to wonder what was going on in the minds of his two best friends. In one morning they had transformed from likable simpletons into total jerks. Tears begin to well up in his eyes. Things needed to be straightened out, and fast. As angry as he was at Darryl and Dwayne, Derek knew it was his duty, as their friend, to step in and help guide them back to a world of sensibility. The question was, how?

After a moment of soul searching, Derek realized that the developing problem was more than he could handle on his own. Between eating chips, and guzzling root-beer, he had enough on his plate to worry about. The 'Rick' issue required immediate attention. Who could he turn to? Who could possibly help him? All the roosters believed Rick blew sunshine out of his cloacae, and the hens were all comb over wattles in love with him. Sadly, Derek realized that he was out of choices.

His gizzards began to turn as he considered the only remaining option. There was only one rooster with the power and status to bring common sense back to his mindless buddies. Rescuing his friends from their own stupidity would mean cashing in his pride to do so. Begrudgingly, Derek set off in search of his brother.

* * *

"Let me get this straight," Mr. Stevens asked with a chuckle. "*You* are coming to *me* for assistance? Me, the brother you have picked on and tormented his whole life? You have to be kidding?" Mr. Stevens had been chomping down on some leftover kibble at the food trough when his brother tracked him down, begging for his help.

"Believe me Dirk, I wish I was kidding," Derek replied sheepishly. "I would rather have my wattles air-nailed to a fence post than ask for your help, but I am all out of options."

"Gee, thanks for the vote of confidence," Mr. Stevens retorted, shaking his head in disgust. "Glad I can serve as your last resort. What can *I* possibly do for *you* Derek? Do you want me to lower my head so you can make fun of my comb? Maybe I could stand here, perfectly still, and let you kick me in the giblets?"

Derek was growing tired of his brother's sarcasm and his impatience began to show. "Shut-up and listen to me for a minute Dirk," Derek shot back, "I need-"

"That's Mr. Stevens to you," Dirk interrupted. "I'm in charge of this coop and will be addressed as mister. How many times do I have to-?" he stopped mid-sentence, voice trailing off.

Derek's entire demeanour had suddenly changed. The crusty façade, the cockiness, and the trademark potato chip swagger were gone. Derek's beak began to quiver. Then, to the surprise of them both, he started to cry.

"Can we just cut out this mister crap for a minute?" he stammered through a stream of tears. "I need your assistance Dirk. As a brother, and as leader of this coop, please help me!"

This was the moment Dirk Stevens had been waiting for his entire life. After all the years of torment, the tables had finally turned. His brother was now the one seeking mercy. His first instinct was to grease Derek and his dirty mullet for being a crying sissy. This is what Derek would have undoubtedly done to him. However, after careful consideration, Mr. Stevens decided to put revenge on hold. There would be plenty of time for that later. His brother was in obvious distress and in need of help. As leader of the coop it was his duty to at least hear what Derek had to say. With an exasperated sigh, and a nod of his head, Mr. Stevens agreed. "Alright bro, tell me what's going on."

Derek looked up at his brother with a look of both shock and gratitude. "Thanks," he offered before verbally walking Mr. Stevens through the details of the morning. He started out calmly, but grew hot under the wattles as he angrily described how Rick and his two best friends had spent the morning smoking together. He went on to share Darryl and Dwayne's desire to become the stars of Rick's Cockle-Doodle-Doo-Tube videos. His brother carefully listened as he spun his tale of woe.

"You know, I tried to give him the benefit of the doubt, being new and all," Mr. Stevens admitted. "However, I think it's time that Rick and I had a little chat. Sounds to me like he needs an attitude adjustment."

Derek nodded. He could not have agreed more.

Truth be told, Mr. Stevens was a little nervous about confronting and having a chat with Rick. His tattoos, leather, and comb piercing were all characteristics of a fairly tough customer. Nevertheless, all fears aside, as leader of the coop he had the responsibility of looking out for the well-being of all the other chickens. It was his duty to seek out Rick and encourage him to change his ways.

"All right Derek, lets go find him," Mr. Stevens suggested. "I'll check over by the henhouse and feed station, you take the Rooster Club and back section of the coop. If you come across him first, let our little friend know that he and I need to have a serious conversation."

Derek agreed, and the two brothers set off in their different directions, both on a mission to bring order back to the barnyard. Derek decided to check things out in the Rooster Club first. He knew Darryl and Dwayne planned on being there to shoot their stupid video so it seemed like an intelligent, first choice. As he approached, a loud ruckus could be heard, coming from within. Moving closer he realized that the noises came from a large mob of clucking roosters.

"C'mon Dwayne, smack him in the beak," shouted an overly enthusiastic cockerel.

"Get him Darryl. Plow him in the wattles," chirped another excitedly.

"C'mon Dwayne, get him in the wing lock and smash in his keel!"

"Screw that! Pull his comb Darryl! Tug his tail feathers! Grab his gizzards!"

Derek's eyes moved across the enclosure until he saw what the commotion was all about; his two best friends engaged in a violent exchange of wing-to-wing combat. He stood in shock for a moment as his mind processed the despicable scene. Then, moving as quickly as his overhanging belly would allow, he thrust himself through the throng of onlookers, jumped between the two combatants, and pried Darryl and Dwayne apart.

Holding each back by their keels Derek lit into his two best buds. "What in the name of Mother-Cluck is wrong with you two idiots? Why are you pounding the snot out of each other?"

Before either could reply, a strong wing reached around from behind and took a firm grip of Derek's wattles. "Perhaps I can shed some light on the situation for you," Rick sneered, tightening his grip. "You are going to pay for this little interruption, you cholesterol infested dingle berry? You just cost me some hard earned kibble."

Derek stared back at Rick, both frightened and confused. "Kibble? What are you talking about," he asked.

"I'm talking about the fight you just broke up, you dumb son of a hen!" Rick squawked.

"What? You mean the fight, just now, where my two best friends were trying to kill one another?" Derek chirped back.

Rick growled back at the oversized rooster. "No you stupid clucker. I mean the fight your two best friends were putting on as a dry run for our new business venture. Look around nimrod," he continued, motioning with his wing to the angry group of onlookers. "Every one of these fine lads came here to watch a quality cockfight. We were practicing for our big debut on Cockle-Doodle-Doo-Tube tonight. Filming a preview, so to speak. If we can't advertise our wares, we certainly can't sell our fights to other barns."

"What are you talking about?" Derek asked in disbelief, not fully grasping the situation.

"I'm talking about you, sticking your greasy mullet, and potato chip gut where they don't belong." He jabbed Derek in the belly button with his wing. "This was the practice run for our big broadcast. Cockfighting on Cockle-Doodle-Doo-Tube is going to be a huge profit-maker. Other barns will pay top kibble to watch a good scrap."

"Let me get this straight," Derek said feebly, attempting to summarize the conversation. "You are staging cockfights, and selling them to other barns on Cockle-Doodle-Doo-Tube?"

"Basically," Rick replied with a shrug of his wings. "And, of course, there is a little in-house wagering that goes along with it as well."

The shocked expression on Derek's face grew as he processed the last tidbit of information. "Our own fellow roosters are betting on the fights?" he cried out in disbelief. Rick responded with a cheeky little nod.

Derek was stunned, unsure of what to say next. On top of smoking, and acting like idiots, Darryl and Dwayne were now involved in an elaborate cockfighting scheme. *What was going on in the coop?* Before he could come up with an answer, his two best friends started in on him.

"I can't believe you did that Derek," Dwayne piped up, waddling over and giving him a shove. "Darryl and I are trying to become icons in the cockfighting world. Why don't you go have another bag of chips and leave us alone to chase our dreams?"

Derek stared at his friend, stunned. "You and Darryl are supposed to be friends," he chided. "Friends aren't supposed to spend their free time kicking the spit out of each other."

Dwayne smacked Derek across the face with his wing. "It's a business you idiot. We plow each other a few times, bloody a comb here, break a wing there, and then head back to the Rooster Club with a beak full of kibble. The roosters love it, the hens dig it, and we become stars. It's all part of the show. Darryl and I *are* still friends, you chip-inhaling ninny. It's you I'm not so sure about . . ."

Derek was speechless. *What was he saying?*

"C'mon Rick, I need a smoke," Darryl said angrily. "Get me away from this tool!"

"Yeah! Me too," Dwayne added spitefully. "This loser needs to get out of my sight before I freak out and smash his beak in."

"Great idea fellas. Time to let this meatball get back to his busy day of doing nothing," Rick replied, hauling off and slugging Derek in the gut. "See you later tubby," he growled. "We're out of here."

Struggling to catch his breath, Derek called out to the three as they headed to the yard for their smoke break. "Before you guys go, I have a message to pass along." He paused and pointed his wing at the ringleader. "Specifically, it's *you* I have the message for Rick. Mr. Stevens wants to have a chat with *you*, ASAP."

"Moi?" Rick replied sarcastically spreading his wings wide. "Whatever could the coop loser, er, I mean leader want from good old Ricky-poo?"

Derek stared at Rick with disdain. "He wants to discuss your flagrant disregard of the rules, regulations and policies of this barnyard!" he shot back.

"Sounds good to me," Rick said with a chuckle. "I'd love to talk to our exalted leader about the asinine rules that govern this place. Things are going to change around here in the very near future. Soon it'll be me running the show."

"Good luck with that," Derek replied smugly. "My brother saved every chicken in this coop from being plucked, roasted and eaten. You think they are going to listen to a rooster they hardly even know?"

Rick glared angrily and waddled back towards Derek. "I think these roosters are all desperate for a change, begging for one really," he snarled, suddenly lashing out with both wings, shoving Derek to the ground.

Flashing an evil little grin, Rick continued. "Actually, it is *I* who has the message; a message for your prissy little brother. Perhaps you'd be kind enough to pass it along for me?" Derek hesitantly nodded, fearing for his life. "You let that sorry sack of sheep spew know that he has a choice to make. Either he voluntarily relinquishes control of this coop to me, or I shall have him banished for life."

Still sprawled out on the ground, Derek glared back at Rick, "Mr. Stevens will *never* pass over control of this coop to a lowlife degenerate like you. Not in a million years. He'd rather eat his own puke. Contrary to what you may think, my brother isn't scared of you," Derek shot back.

Rick kicked out his foot and placed it strategically on Derek's throat, pressing him to the ground, blocking his airway. "He *will* be scared of me, my rotund little friend. You can take that cheque to the bank and cash it right now. If you're as smart as I think you are, you'll take your overhanging gut and half eaten bag of chips, find your brother, and convince him to make the smart decision. Otherwise we'll see how long he lasts out in the wild with the coyotes."

With a gleam in his eye, Rick gave his leg a sudden jerk, his foot catching Derek square in the beak. "Now, if you'll excuse me," he continued coolly. "You've wasted enough of my precious time. I have an appointment with a pack of cigarettes and my two new best friends. Sayonara, clucker!"

Five

After her brief social encounter with Rick at the food trough, Gladys had taken a short walk to de-fluster herself. All she could think about was the handsome hellion in the leather vest. He was such a luscious hunk; so irresistible it made her weak in the giblets. She imagined him wrapping his muscular wings around her and embracing in a prolonged beak-lock behind the barn. How desperately she hoped he shared her feelings of lust.

Arriving back at the henhouse, Gladys noticed the other hens were staring at her with a variety of odd expressions. *They must be so jealous,* she thought to herself, adding a little swagger to her waddle. *And really, why wouldn't they be? She was the only hen to have had an actual encounter with Rick. The others could eat their hearts out. Rick was all hers.* Gladys was certain that it was only a matter of time before she officially became, Mrs. Rick.

It was as she came up to her stall that she understood the reasons behind all the puzzling glances. Pictures. Pictures of her. Pictures of her in a variety of unflattering situations. Pictures that had been posted publicly on her Face-Beak wall for all to see. The other hens looked away, snickering to one another, as Gladys quickly inspected the incriminating posts. Her heart sank. If Rick saw these, her chances with him would be over.

Her gaze locked on a single photo. It featured her, eyes bugged out, straining to pass an exceptionally large egg. Gladys remembered the morning Janet had taken the picture like it was yesterday. Afterwards they had giggled together, making jokes about the constipated expression on her face. It was a special moment between friends. A moment that all of a sudden, wasn't so special anymore. Her eyes continued to roam across the stall wall, examining the other pictures that were now up on public display. Her wattles turned red with embarrassment at the one that showed her fluffing up her keel feathers to make her chest look bigger.

As bad as the pictures were, they paled in comparison to the written messages. Mean messages. Unflattering messages. Messages that divulged many of her personal secrets. She had only shared these secrets with one other hen thus responsibility for the horrible attack was clear. Janet! In a moment of extreme jealousy she had publicly posted the pictures and mean messages for the whole world to see. As Gladys slowly read through each post, her resentment and feelings of betrayal grew greater and greater.

'Cornmeal gives Gladys gas.'

'Gladys has under-wing, perspiration issues.'

'Gladys over-preens her tail.'

'Gladys is fat.'

'Gladys has rooster parts.'

'Gladys is the egg that should have been scrambled.'

Reading through each message, Gladys grew more and more upset. Tears of humiliation streamed down her face. She couldn't believe such personal information had been posted so publicly. All her dirty laundry had been hung out for every-fowl to see. Hardest to digest was the fact that this cruel, defenseless attack had come from her very best friend. A hen she trusted like a sister. A hen, who just this morning, had posted a picture of the two of them as BFFs.

Making matters worse, and complicating the situation further, were the 'likes'. Many hens had anonymously ticked off the box that indicated personal agreement with what had been posted. Not only had Janet betrayed her; but it seemed many of her friends had jumped on the bandwagon as well. Although she had no idea which friends they were. Gladys turned to find a crowd of nosey hens staring back at her, anxiously waiting to gauge her reaction. Janet stood off to one side of the group, wings crossed in front of her and a smug expression on her beak.

"Why?" Gladys asked woefully. "Why, did you do this to me?"

Janet took a step forward. "Why?" she replied. "Why do you think?"

"I don't have a clue," Gladys sobbed. "I honestly have no idea. But, after all the humiliation you've just put me through, I think I have the right to know. You should at least have the decency to tell me what I've done to deserve, this," she pointed to her Face-Beak wall. "We are best friends."

"*Were* best friends," Janet corrected. "You threw that out the window when you started throwing yourself at *my* man!"

"What are you talking about?" Gladys replied defensively. "I didn't throw myself at him. I went up and spoke to him, fowl to fowl. You could have done the same thing, just as easily. Besides, who says he's *your* man anyway."

"Shut your beak Gladys! You're nothing more than a cheap floozy. A cheap floozy who *had* to have Rick, no matter the cost!" Janet shot back. "You chased after him without once considering that maybe one of us gals wanted a piece of him too. You fluffed up your keel feathers and dolled up your comb like a five-cent doxy. Then you waddled your oversized rump out to the trough so you could seduce him and keep him all for yourself. You are a selfish hen Gladys. You always put your own interests before everything else. Quite simply, I'm tired of it." Janet then motioned to the other hens. "*We're* tired of it! All of us!"

Gladys stared back at Janet with a blank gaze. "All I did was have a twenty second conversation with him. That's it. If you had such a problem with what I was doing, why didn't you just talk to me, or send a private message to my nest?" Gladys cried. "Those pictures are so humiliating. The secrets you shared with everyone were heart felt confessions that I made to you, my best friend, in confidence. They were things I could only talk about with you. Now every hen in the henhouse knows about my perspiration issues, my rooster parts *and* my gas problem.

I trusted you! You were like a sister to me! How could you betray me like this?''

For a split second, Janet felt a slight pang of guilt. There was definitely some truth to what Gladys was saying. Because of her posts, Gladys *had* become the laughing stock of the barnyard. But then her thoughts shifted to Rick. Beautiful, chain-smoking Rick. Janet had to have him. If Gladys was going to stand in her way then she would have to accept the repercussions of doing so. All was fair in love and war. And this was love.

"You just watch yourself Gladys. There are plenty more where these posts came from," Janet threatened, pointing a wing at the embarrassing pictures. "Stay away from my rooster. Got it? Rick is mine. M. I. N. E. I am prettier than you, thinner than you, and smarter than you. Once he finds out that you're nothing more than a dolled-up, gas-infested, kibble-chomping hussy, you won't stand a chance.''

Janet's stream of nasty words caused something inside Gladys to snap. Like a switch had been flipped, her emotions shifted from feelings of weeping sorrow to those of fiery rage. "Maybe it's *you* that's going to have to watch herself you rotten tramp!'' she squealed at her former BFF. The tears had stopped and anger took their place. "I have dirt too, you dog-faced trollop. Everything you told me in confidence back when we *were* friends is now fair game. Keep your guard up you barrel-chested, two-faced, tart!''

"Bring it on you filthy harlot!" Janet shot back, taking the challenge. "I'm not the least bit scared of you. You don't have the wattles to compete with me!"

"Oh I've got the wattles, bimbo! Don't think I won't tear you a new one," Gladys raged. "Don't! Think! I! Won't! If you think I'm going to sit here and take your spit, think again you soiled strumpet!"

"Bite me, you vindictive vamp!" Janet taunted. "Go lay an egg! You've got nothing on me!"

"We'll see about that, you gutless sack of cow cud! Mark my words, you will regret the day you hid behind Face-Beak to fight your battles," Gladys threatened, flipping a middle feather at her former confidante.

"Oooooh, I'm so scared," Janet squawked back sarcastically, flipping up a middle feather of her own.

"You will be when I pluck you alive for not shutting that cratered beak of yours!" Gladys retorted. "Pluck! You! Alive!"

Both scowled at each other with looks of pure hatred. When eye contact finally broke, the two indignant hens turned and stomped back to their respective stalls. The rest of the hens all shifted uneasily. What were they to do? Some decided to follow Janet while the others tagged along behind Gladys. Each would have an angry tale to tell after the big squabble, and they couldn't wait to listen. There was nothing quite like a good gossip session to keep things vibrant in the henhouse.

Sandra Thompson had taken in the entire confrontation from the confines of her stall. She was both shocked and dismayed at what she had witnessed. It was common knowledge that anytime a group of hens separated into cliques, the end result was never positive. And that was exactly what was happening. A glance at the High Jinx Meter told her all she needed to know. The needle had jumped from yellow to orange over the course of the past few minutes. They were now one step closer to disaster. Sandra needed to find Dirk Stevens immediately. He was their only hope at resolving the hen drama before total chaos ensued.

*   *   *

At the exact same moment, both Sandra and Derek crashed upon Mr. Stevens as he lurked around the yard in search of Rick. The two smashed into him, sending him tumbling to the ground. Each began rambling off in loud, inaudible squawks. The level of concern in their tones was an obvious indication that something horrible was amiss.

"Whoa!" Mr. Stevens interjected, throwing a wing into the air as he slowly rose and brushed himself off. "Slow down. I can't understand either one of you. One at a time, please, so I can actually process your words." He nodded towards Sandra. "You start."

Sandra took a deep breath and began describing the high jinx going on in the henhouse. "Well, the hens are all worked up in a tizzy over this, this, this Rick character," she stammered, shaking her head in disgust. "They are actually competing for him. Dolling themselves up like ten-cent trolls to vie for his attention. Both Janet and Gladys are out of control. Janet just posted a whole bunch of personal pictures of Gladys on Face-Beak. Gladys is irate, and plotting her revenge as we speak."

"But, Janet and Gladys are friends." Mr. Stevens pointed out. "Best friends."

Sandra took another deep breath before continuing. "Not anymore. Far from it in fact. To make matters worse, the hens have now divided; some following Gladys, the others following Janet. And we all know what happens when groups of girls band together. Ugh! Things are going downhill so quickly, the High Jinx Meter has already hit orange."

"Orange? That's preposterous! If this keeps up it will hit red by evening feed!" Mr. Stevens exclaimed in surprise. He paused for a moment to fully absorb Sandra's news, rubbing his head with his wings. "What a nightmare!" Both Derek and Sandra nodded in agreement. Life in the coop was quickly spinning out of control.

Mr. Stevens looked to his brother. "How about you Derek? Do you have anything to report? Did you have any luck finding Rick? I looked all over but found neither hide nor feather of him."

Derek nodded his head solemnly, "Ya. I, uh, I found him."

Mr. Stevens carefully examined his brother's body language, "And?" he asked cautiously.

"And, things are not very good Dirk. In fact, truth be told, they're terrible." Derek replied sadly. "Rick is staging cockfights in the Rooster Club with plans to record and sell them on Cockle-Doodle-Doo-Tube."

"What!" Mr. Stevens bellowed. "Cockfights? Cockfights in my chicken coop? That's impossible! This is a cockfight free coop. Are you sure I heard you correctly?"

"Yes, you heard me just fine," Derek continued. "The first two fighters were Darryl and Dwayne. They were having a 'practice' bout. When I arrived they were busy kicking the living dung out of one another. I jumped in to break it up, and instead of thanking me; they cursed me out, basically telling me I wasn't their friend anymore. Their cloacae are all tied in knots because I ruined their chance to become stars." There was a pause in Derek's explanation as he exhaled slowly. "But that's not the worst part."

"What pray tell is the worst part, Derek?" Mr. Stevens asked, cringing in anticipation of his brother's response.

"Those who aren't fighting will be busy betting on the outcome. They are placing wagers, of kibble, on these stupid cockfights. Rick, no doubt, will be taking a cut off of every wager," Derek explained angrily. "He's set up an organized gambling ring, right here, in *our* Rooster Club!"

"Gambling? In my coop? That's impossible," Mr. Stevens exclaimed angrily. "This is a gambling free coop."

"It's also a smoke free and cockfighting free coop, but that hasn't stopped him," Sandra said frankly. "It's obvious that this tyrant has no regard whatsoever for the rules and regulations of our barnyard."

Mr. Stevens went red in the wattles with anger. "This guy has only been here a few hours and he's already turned the coop upside down. Arghhhh!" Calming himself slightly, he continued to press Derek for information. "Were you at least able to pass on my message?" he asked. "Did you let him know I want to speak with him?"

"Oh, I passed your message along alright, right after he squeezed my wattles, stomped on my throat and kicked me in the beak," Derek clucked angrily. "He replied with a message of his own."

"Do tell," Mr. Stevens requested curiously. "Is he ready for our little talk?"

Derek sighed deeply, "Oh, he's ready Dirk. Rick seems to believe that *he'll* be leading the ranks around here in the very near future. He says you can either join in, or be banished forever. He is expecting an answer by the evening feed."

A look of concern washed across Mr. Stevens' face. "And if I don't like either of those options?" he replied nervously, voice cracking.

Derek lowered his head sadly. "He said if you didn't choose on your own, he'd make the decision *for* you."

Mr. Stevens slowly sat and began fanning himself nervously with a wing. Sandra came over and gently rubbed his saddle. "Don't worry, there's no way the other chickens will support Rick as leader of this coop. Not after you risked your life to save them," she reassured, reminding Mr. Stevens of his previous heroics. "No way will they forgot the debt of gratitude they still owe you."

"Sandra, I hate to burst your bubble," Derek interrupted. "But, after what I just witnessed, I'd say they already *have* forgotten. He has the hens all tarting themselves up while the roosters smoke, fight and gamble. No matter how we look at it, Dirk is screwed! Rick has only been here since breakfast and is already making claims that he's going to make this coop the most exciting place on the planet. The other chickens are fully buying in to his illusions of grandeur."

After hearing Derek's explanation, Mr. Stevens was even more unnerved. He *had* lost control of the coop. *His* coop. If he didn't act quickly all his credibility would be lost. The time to act had arrived. Standing around and allowing his fellow fowl to be brainwashed and bullied was unacceptable. It was time to rise up against the demonic fiend that was threatening his peaceful sanctuary. The time to stand strong and give a cluck, was now!

If Mr. Stevens failed to use his influence as leader, mass chaos would reign. *He* was still in charge of the coop and there was no way some tattooed stranger was going to waltz in and take that honour away from him. "I look forward to this meeting at the evening feed," Mr. Stevens stated strongly, his confidence returning. "The time has come for Rick and I to have a discussion, rooster to rooster. It's time he learned to show a little respect for authority."

*   *   *

As Mr. Stevens continued analyzing the dire situation with Derek and Sandra, a meeting of different proportions was taking place back at the Rooster Club. "It's time I took over this sinking ship?" Rick declared to the others, taking a long haul off a freshly lit cigarette.

The other roosters looked around at each other in total confusion. "What ship?" Dwayne piped up. "I don't see no water."

Rick shook his head and stared at Dwayne in wonder. "I know there's no water, you moron. I was speaking metaphorically," he sneered, a hint of disgust evident in his cackle.

"Oh," Dwayne quickly replied, his wattles reddening with embarrassment. "I knew that. D'uh."

Rick ignored Dwayne's stupidity for the moment and continued along his train of thought, "We need to spice things up around here boys; eliminate the domestic boredom. Roosters have a lifespan of about eight years. Do we really want to spend our short time on this planet waddling around doing whatever the farmer dictates?" He paused momentarily for contemplation. "Not me boys. No way. I don't want to live a life where the only things I have to look forward to are eating stale corn niblets and passing a little gas in my stall. I want to live an exciting life, in an exciting place. A place *we* can all be proud to call *our* home." Rick radiated a confident air of self-assurance that mesmerized his simple audience.

"What about Mr. Stevens," Darryl asked innocently. "He just took over the coop from Mr. Thompson. I'm not sure he's gonna want to give up his place on the perch just yet. *And*, I highly doubt he'll be jumping on board with some of these great new activities. He doesn't really have much when it comes to a sense of fun."

Rick chuckled, "Well Darryl, you make a good point, you really do. Mr. Stevens wouldn't know a good time if it came up and plucked his tail feathers. But, thankfully there is only *one* of him and *dozens* of us. When we all stand as one and demonstrate our commitment to creating a more dynamic living environment, he will have no choice but to see things *our* way."

"And if he doesn't?" a young Rhode Island Red piped up from the back of the crowd.

"Then we will make the decision for him," Rick snarled.

"You mean like overthrow his leadership?" Darryl probed.

"That will be happening regardless," Rick replied ruthlessly. "I'm talking about tossing his sorry saddle right out the door; banishing him from the barnyard forever."

Rick carefully examined the reactions of his fellow fowl as they digested this last idea. He saw some heads begin to nod while others continued to waver with stunned looks on their faces. "If Mr. Stevens is allowed to continue in his current leadership role, life will continue to suck. If you're tired of rolling out of your nests at the crack of dawn because some rooster has decided it's time, cluck for change!" he commanded in a strong voice.

A positive murmur, and low level of clucking began to rise from the audience.

"Aren't you tired of living the same dull routine every day in this stinky, crap infested pen? I have only been here for a couple of hours and already hate it!"

Several 'yeah's' trickled out of the crowd, encouraging Rick to ramp up his motivational monologue. "What about living a life of freedom? A life where every rooster is able to exercise his right to be an individual, instead of having his independence thwarted by the expectations of the barnyard? What about living a life where every rooster has full control of his own destiny?"

"Yeah!" the roosters shouted in unison, unaware at this point what they were even cheering for. All they knew was that Rick spoke with a passion unlike any-fowl they had ever heard before. He also used intelligent sounding words. There may have been confusion in his message but one fact was crystal clear. Rick needed to take charge. As far as they were concerned he was their only shot at a better life. Whatever it took to assist their new messiah, they were prepared to give.

"Boys," he announced. "It's time we stand up for what is right. It's time we stand up for *our* rights. If it is freedom you want, stand tall with me now!"

"YEAH!" the roosters squawked as loud as their little beaks would allow.

Rick stood back and crossed his wings, a smug expression spread across his face. "Tonight at the evening feed, Mr. Stevens shall be shown how a real coop is run! Tonight this coop shall become *our* dominion!"

"What about the hens?" Darryl asked, with slight concern in his voice. "What if they don't buy into this new philosophy?"

"Leave that to me," Rick replied, flashing an evil smile.

Six

The hens were the first to arrive for the evening feed, and their mood could be summed up in one word: Fowl. It had been a quiet afternoon in the henhouse following the heated exchange between Janet and Gladys. Not a single egg had been laid. Rather, the young ladies had spent their free time preening, and dolling themselves up for Rick.

Instead of congregating together, the ladies sauntered up in the two individual entourages of Janet and Gladys. Neither group mingled with the other, choosing to huddle together angrily with their wings crossed and beaks pursed instead. Hen drama was running rampant throughout the barnyard. What had started as a simple rift between two friends had quickly escalated into a much larger issue. Allies had been chosen, sides had been drawn, and continued hostility seemed unavoidable. Hens who barely knew either of the two combatants now found themselves wattle-deep in the ridiculous dispute.

"Look at Cindy!" a young hen named Jackie pointed out to Gladys. "She's standing next to Janet like they've been best friends for years. Humph! What a saddle-stabber!"

"I know," an older hen named Annie added. "Check out Jody over there trying to be all bestie with Janet. She's got herself all fluffed up like a bloated whale. What a flake-tool. I can't stand that hussy!"

Ironically, just that morning, Jody and Annie had been BFFs of their own. As the anger began to swell on both sides, Rick made his grand entrance, shuffling up to the girls with his usual confident swagger. The other roosters followed behind; far enough to give Rick an ample amount of breathing room as he addressed the hens.

"Ladies," he boomed in his deepest, sexiest voice. "I have an announcement to make?" He gave his tail feathers a little wiggle, a move that caused one young pullet to faint. Hearts fluttered, gizzards quivered, legs turned to mush. Rick had arrived, and he had something to say.

"This evening, my precious lasses, I am here to share a proposal with you." All the hens listened intently, momentarily forgetting their issues. Proposal? Sounded exciting. Heads tilted, beaks opened, and drool began to ooze as Rick launched into his spiel.

"First off, let me ask you all a question?" he began, with a charismatic smile that caused more than a few keels to palpitate. "How many of you sweet young things are tired of running the same routine, day, after day, after clucking day?"

A few heads bobbed, a few wings rose, and a few chests were thrust out in hopes of garnering a second glance from the divine degenerate. "Imagine a coop where life is what *you* want it to be!" he continued. "Imagine a coop where *you* decide your daily activities and control your own daily routine."

A few hens clucked their approval. "Does this mean not sitting around all day laying eggs for Farmer Johnston?" a young pullet questioned. "Because quite frankly, I get so tired pinching those dang things out."

"Ya, me too," declared another. "And judging by the pics on Gladys' Face-Beak stall, she'd like a break from the extra strain as well." This brought howls of laughter from Janet's camp. Gladys scowled in disgust, her face reddening with embarrassment.

Rick ignored the comments and continued with his delivery. "Ladies, I want to take this coop and turn it into something spectacular. A place full of fun and excitement where *we* can all enjoy the freedom to do *whatever* we please, *whenever* it pleases us. No more schedules and no more tedious daily routines!"

The hens all nodded, many clucking their approval. "In theory it sounds good," a young hen named Michelle pointed out. "But, what fun and exciting things will we fill our days with? I mean, look around. This place isn't exactly the most stimulating of environments."

"You'll just have to trust me," Rick replied, flashing a devilish grin. "For starters, how about a dance? Tonight. To celebrate the beginning of a new era here in the barnyard."

A dance! What a terrific idea. All the chickens began to chirp loudly. Rick's smile grew. The coop was as good as his. As predicted, the hens had eaten up his every word. As he prepared to launch into his next pitch, an indignant listener interrupted him.

"Um, excuse me," an angry voice piped up. "It appears as if we have an illegal public gathering formed here." Rick turned to face Mr. Stevens who had snuck up on the group, Sandra and Derek in tow. He stood, wings crossed, with an angry look on his beak. *Ahhhh*, Rick thought to himself. *One more issue to deal with.*

Before Rick could say anything Mr. Stevens was up in his grill. "Now listen carefully you reprobate," he bawled. "If you think these hens are going to shirk their egg laying duties to attend some stupid dance, you've got yourself another think coming." Mr. Stevens poked Rick in the keel sharply with the tip of his wing.

Rick's smile quickly turned into a scowl. "No!" Rick bellowed. "It is *you* that better listen very carefully my little feathered friend." Rick grabbed Mr. Stevens by the wattles and pulled him in so their faces were mere millimeters apart. "*I* am in control of this coop now, dog-breath. We, the fowl, have decided that this barnyard needs a fresh outlook. More fun, more freedom, and less *you*. The decision has been made, you're out and I'm in as leader of this coop." Rick ended his rant by giving Mr. Stevens a two-winged shove.

"You're full of spit!" Mr. Stevens snapped angrily, shoving Rick back. "In order for that to happen there'd need to be an official vote, and you'd legitimately have to win."

Rick sneered and turned to the rest of the chickens, "Okay everyone, let's vote!" he shouted. "All in favour of me taking over as leader of the coop, raise a wing, now." With the exception of Derek and Sandra every wing in the brood shot up in the air.

"I guess the fowl have spoken," Rick chirped with a devilish smile. "You're out Mr. Stevens. Or should I say, you're out, *Dirk*."

Dirk looked around at his fellow fowl, disgusted by their loyalty, or lack thereof. "This isn't over," Dirk squawked back heatedly, pointing his wing at Rick. "Not by a long shot."

"Oh, but I'm afraid it is," Rick laughed. As he spoke, a group of roosters led by Dwayne and Darryl flanked the former leader. "Take him to the quarantine pen boys," Rick commanded. "Lock him up. Let him think about things for the night."

Rick nodded towards Derek and Sandra. "Take those two rejects as well. They came with him thus they can leave with him too." The roosters did as they were told and rounded up the other outcasts.

Once the three had been detained, Rick approached his fuming captives. "You three have a very important decision to make. Either you join in with the new coop philosophy and accept my leadership gracefully, or, you shall be banished from this barnyard forever."

Sandra, who secretly harvested a very nasty temper, could no longer hold in her anger and let loose on Rick. "You are going to destroy this coop!" she screamed angrily. "In one day you've already ruined many of the relationships and friendships these fowl have worked on for years to build." Turning to the rest of the crowd she pleaded, "Don't you see what is happening? Don't you see what he is doing? He is turning you against one another. He's nothing more than a filthy, sociopathic, gizzard-licking, wattle-rubbing, sack of cattle snot. And all of you are falling for his little charade." A set of blank faces stared back at her, not one chicken even remotely moved by her words of wisdom.

"Wow, that was a feisty outburst," Rick laughed in response to Sandra's tirade. "I guess it's safe to say you don't want to be part of my little kingdom here?"

"I'd rather eat three pounds of steaming sheep manure than have anything to do with you," Sandra spat back, seething with anger.

"I'll keep that in mind when I send down your breakfast," Rick replied with a cheeky grin. Quickly turning to the roosters, he laid out his orders. "Get these three ditch pigs out of my sight. Perhaps a night in lock up will help them come to their senses." On his command the three detainees were led away to the quarantine pen. As they disappeared, Rick's mood instantly improved and a smile once again formed on his beak.

"The rest of you," he bellowed out to the remaining crowd. "Grab a quick bite and get ready for tonight's big dance. Let your wattles hang down folks. The time has come to shake our tail feathers with pride!"

Seven

As the hens prepared for the big dance, Rick was the only thing on their simple little minds. As Janet carefully applied a healthy dose of mascara above her eyes, Gladys accosted her, still fired up from their dispute earlier in the day.

"It's all your fault, you vindictive, cross-eyed, cow," Gladys squawked at Janet. "If you hadn't posted that stuff on my Face-Beak wall, Rick and I would be spending the night in each others wings, dancing and rubbing beaks. Now I bet he won't even look at me."

"Oh he'll look at you alright," Janet shot back, "out of scientific wonder."

Gladys reared back and kicked Janet in the cloaca with all her might. Janet recoiled in pain. "It's not like you have a chance either you filthy fowl," she squawked angrily. "With all that mascara you have around your eyes, he's liable to mistake you for a raccoon and run away in fear of being eaten."

"Whatever," Janet chirped back. "You've spent all of thirty seconds with the guy. The only reason he even knows you exist is because you have the unmistakable face of a donkey and the breath of a sewer. I don't know if ugly and stinky are the qualities Rick looks for in a hen."

"Harrumph!" Gladys clucked, throwing her beak in the air snobbishly. "I'm going to powder my nose and preen the feathers on my rump. I'll show Rick what a real piece of tail looks like."

"Ya, a real BIG piece of tail," Janet exclaimed rudely. "I'm sure he'll be really impressed."

"Whatever, Pock Face!" Gladys shot back with a sneer. "It's not like he's going to give you a second glance tonight either. Unless, of course, it's to count all the craters on your beak, you disgusting gnome." Flipping Janet the middle feather Gladys stormed off in a huff, heading back to her own stall.

"Be sure to put on plenty of lipstick," Janet shouted after her. "That way he'll be able to tell your face from your butt!"

*　*　*

As the hens squabbled and prepared for the big dance, the boys relaxed in the Rooster Club, all huddled around the coop's newest icon. "So the way I see it boys," Rick boasted, "things are going to be a whole lot different with me in charge. I'll be making the rules from here on in."

"What sort of rules will there be?" a young cockerel asked.

Rick approached the little rooster, stared him straight in the eye and spoke in a soft, uncharacteristically warm tone. "Well little friend, as you undoubtedly know, my philosophy is one that supports an individual's rights to independence and freedom." He reared back his head and bellowed. "There shall be no rules!" The roosters all wing slapped one another in excitement. No longer would strict regulations strip them of their individuality, whatever that meant.

Rick went silent and the roosters all gathered in close. "Fellas, I think it's time we talked a little bit more about

Cockle-Doodle-Doo-Tube." A creepy look swept across his face as he spoke. "I'm thinking if we play it just right, we can make ourselves a pile of extra kibble."

"How?" Darryl asked, snapping a fresh cigarette into his beak. "How can recording a bunch of fights make us kibble?"

Rick smiled, "I'm glad you asked Darryl. That is a very good question." Darryl beamed as Rick praised him in front of the group. "Let me explain the principal of supply and demand to you lads. Do you remember that fight we recorded this afternoon?" he asked.

"I sure do," Darryl replied goofily. "I still have the black eye to prove it." True enough, his left eye had swollen almost entirely shut from where Dwayne had caught him with a mean right jab.

"You see boys, it's all about being able to provide something that no one else can. Right now, we can record a bunch of fights and then sell the recordings to other barns for viewing on Cockle-Doodle-Doo-Tube. The other barns that pick them up can start their own betting rings, and make their own kibble from the fights just like we do. Right now there is a huge demand out there for new rooster entertainment. If we can supply that entertainment, we'll be rich. All we have to do is ensure that we put together a good product, and, have lots of variety. If we can serve up an endless supply of quality cockfights, we'll be rich! As we are the first ones out of the gate on this little venture, there will be no competition from the other barns. *All* the kibble will be ours!."

"Can *we* still bet on the fights?" Dwayne asked.

"Absolutely, that's half the fun. You can bet all you want with no worries. So much kibble will be coming in as a result of this new business enterprise; there'll be no risk of going broke. Boys, as I see it, this is a risk free investment."

The roosters all looked around at one another with big grins. Supply and demand sounded like a great system indeed! Gambling, fighting, extra kibble, what could be better? "What do you say amigos? Are you in?" Rick asked with a greasy grin.

The response was unanimous. Every rooster in the coop was sold on the idea. Rick was a visionary. The more fights they had, the more fights they'd sell. The more fights they sold, the more kibble they earned. The more kibble they earned, the more kibble they could wager on the fights. It was a brilliant scheme. So brilliant that most of the roosters were ready to start fighting right away. They all wanted a piece of the action.

"If you guys are okay with everything, I suggest we get started after tonight's dance," Rick recommended, to a round of loud and approving chirps. "The quicker we get started, the sooner the kibble starts rolling in. All we need is a couple of volunteers to be the first to do battle. Any takers?"

The roosters looked around at one another, sizing up the competition. After a moment or so, a tiny cockerel stepped forward. "My name is Marty and it would be an honour to fight in the battle tonight. I may be slight of size, but don't let that deceive you. I am a feisty little fowl and will take on *any* rooster in this coop."

Rick nodded his approval, impressed at the young fighter's spunk. He handed the mini rooster a cigarette. "Good for you little thug, good for you. Anyone care to accept Marty's challenge?"

Craig, a large, overdeveloped Delaware raised a wing. "I'll take the challenge!" he clucked. "What's more, for all of you planning to place a wager, I am guaranteeing a very clear and decisive victory."

A hush settled over the group. The Delaware was easily five times as large as the young cockerel. Marty didn't stand a chance. He was a dead bird clucking. "It's on!" Rick stated with excitement, tossing a cigarette to Craig. "Meet back here immediately following the dance and we'll set things up. Don't forget to place your bets gentlemen, and remember, the house only takes ninety percent. With me, of course, representing the house."

The boys clucked with excitement as they hurried back to their stalls to make themselves presentable for the dance.

As they slapped cologne under their wattles and dabbed deodorant under their wings, each took a moment to reflect and be thankful. Thankful that Rick had descended upon their coop. Life had improved so much since he'd arrived. A night of dancing followed by a spectacular cockfight was indeed the perfect evening. Quite possibly, this would be the best night *ever* in the history of Farmer Johnston's barnyard. Rick was that special something they had been waiting for their entire lives.

*   *   *

At the lock up, Dirk, Derek and Sandra all sat on hay bales with glum looks spread across their beaks. In the background they could hear the music of Twisted Fencepost blasting into the evening sky as the chickens danced the night away. Dejectedly, they discussed their limited options.

"I don't like the way Rick operates but if I am banished from the coop, where will I go?" Derek asked out loud. "I can't exactly fend for myself in the wild. Not without my chips."

"But Derek, we can't stay here and live under Rick's regime," Sandra replied. "I'd rather take my chances with the wild than live under the rule of that greasy clucker."

"No one is going anywhere," Dirk interjected. "We won't be following his rules, and we certainly aren't going to be banished from our own coop."

"But how can we avoid it? How in the name of Mother-Cluck are we going to get out of this pickle?" Derek asked, clearly out of ideas. "What is our plan of attack?"

Dirk stared back at his brother with a blank expression on his beak. "As soon as I think of something, you two will be the first to know," he replied, in a tone that didn't exactly instill confidence in his co-captives "The first to know," he repeated, voice tailing off.

*   *   *

By ten o'clock the dance was in full swing. All the roosters and hens were thrashing and grinding in the barnyard under the light of a full moon. Rick mingled through the crowd speaking briefly to each of his minions. As the new leader, it was his job to at least *appear* interested in the daily lives of his fellow fowl.

Janet and her cronies stayed well away from Gladys and her cohort. Both tried to individually attract Rick's attention with a series of seductive tail gyrations and saddle shimmies, but he was far too caught up in working the masses to notice either one of their efforts. Gladys' blood began to boil as she took Rick's inattentiveness as a sign of rejection. She had spent so much time applying extra lipstick, preening her tail, and stuffing her keel feathers, yet hadn't received as much as a second glance from the delightful dissident.

In her mind, the reason was obvious. Rick must have seen the pictures on Face-Beak. The look on her face as she strained to pass that especially large Omega—3 must have turned his gizzards. She had Janet to thank for that embarrassment. How she hated that dragon-faced, saddle-stabber. Realizing her chances with Rick had diminished to none, Gladys decided payback time had finally arrived.

She chose the moment Janet became engrossed in conversation with another pullet to quietly slip out of the crowd. If she couldn't have Rick, Janet wouldn't either. As the music blasted into the star-filled night, Gladys headed back to the henhouse to exact her revenge. The needle on the High Jinx Meter now pushed hard red. An event of catastrophic proportions was unavoidable.

Eight

It was early morning when the chickens finally decided to shut down the music and head back to their nests. Everyfowl left feeling alive and vibrant. The night had been spectacular; shirking all responsibilities to dance, and eat, and twist, and drink. The water trough had been filled three times over the course of the evening to rehydrate the posse of sweating poultry. Two roosters even snuck into the feed hut and pilfered a little extra cornmeal for a mid-night snack, much to the delight of all in attendance. All in all, it had been a momentous occasion, a party for the ages so to speak.

As the roosters and hens said their final goodnights and headed their separate ways, energy continued to buzz in the air. Although it was hours past normal nest time, the chickens were restless, most still hyped up from the fabulous barnyard bash. In the henhouse it took about eleven seconds for all the extra energy to be put to use as the hen drama finally boiled over.

"WTF????" Janet screamed. "What! The! Fowl! Is! This?" She stood, beak agape, staring into her stall, or what was left of it. Her entire enclosure had been destroyed; nest ripped apart, eggs from earlier in the week smashed and smeared all over the walls. Scrawled with yolk in big, bold letters, filling the wall of her tiny home, were the words, "DIE PULLET DIE!"

Several of Janet's followers reacted in anger as they realized that they too had been targeted by the vandals. The mess was horrific. Amidst the damage and destruction, Face-Beak posts had been left. Lots of them. Gladys had kept true to her word, as nothing was left sacred.

"I didn't know you had a pus infection in your wattles," a young hen said to her friend after reading one of the posts. "That's really disgusting."

"Whatever," the friend replied. "It's not as gross as that picture of you eating your own waste."

Through the damage and destruction, an uncontrollable rage began to bubble. The angry hens looked towards their unofficial leader to determine the proper course of action. "Gather around!" Janet barked at her underlings, who followed the orders without question. "Gladys and those other trolls have just written a cheque their bodies can't cash!" she cried out, spreading her wings high over her head. "They have started a war that we are now going to finish!"

"How?" one hen squawked in furor. "What are we going to do?"

"I say we peck their eyes out and spit in the empty sockets!" screeched an indignant pullet. "Thanks to these Face-Beak posts, everyone now knows I missed morning feed the other day because I was constipated."

"Yeah!" cried yet another seething hen. "I say we wing-slap those pullets right in the beaks!"

"Pop 'em in the wattles!"

"Carve out their organs!"

"Let's pluck them alive!"

"Boil them to death!"

"Death to Gladys!"

With each passing suggestion the ideas for revenge grew nastier. Not a single hen was thinking clearly. They were angry and sought immediate vengeance. Only hours earlier they had all been BFFs living in hen harmony. Now they were prepared to fight one another to the death.

"If they want a war?" Janet screamed, like a battalion leader prepping her troops for combat, "then we'll give them a cluck-ing war! It's time we ended this thing once and for all! Attack!"

Janet and her gaggle of irate hens stampeded across the henhouse. The clucking of threats and obscenities was so loud and vile and disgusting, the paint began to peel off the walls. Wings flailed, wattles wavered and combs quivered as the cohort of retribution seeking hens prepared to engage.

Arriving in enemy territory, a hen battle of epic proportions ensued. Tipped off by the noise of the charging chickens, Gladys and her camp were prepared and counterattacked with a push of their own. Eggs from the weekly stockpile were hurled, beaks were slapped, and wattles were squeezed. Squawks and screeches rang loud as eyes were gouged and tail feathers were plucked.

As the hens slapped it out on the henhouse floor, Gladys worked her way through the raging rumble, closing in on her nemesis, Janet. She had a special treat for her former best friend. The treat of pain! Lunging over two comb-pulling hens she grabbed hold of her target with a snarled beak, taking a huge bite out of her saddle. Janet recoiled, screaming in agony.

"Arghhhhhh!" she cried out. "You bit me, you filthy pullet! I can't believe you bit me!"

"Believe it you dirty doxy! Now get back to your side of the barn or I'll take another chomp!" Gladys hissed with rage.

Janet screamed, blood dripping steadily from her wound. "You better sleep with both eyes open tonight Gladys. I'm going to rip your head off and feed it to the sheep!"

"Shut your clucker," Gladys retorted. "I'll slap you senseless, any time, any place. Take your ugly face and the rest of your semi-stunned cluster and beat it!"

"You're going to regret the day you crossed my path you repulsive hussy," Janet screeched angrily. " Mark my words Gladys. I won't rest until I run your oversized rump out of this coop forever." Furiously, she turned and waddled back towards her own end of the pen.

The other rioters took a few final slaps at one another, and shot out a few final chirps and insults before dispersing. Janet's crew followed her out of enemy territory while Gladys and her girls returned to their nests. The fight was over, or more accurately, put on pause for the time being. Undoubtedly, with the continued tensions, the worst was yet to come. As the dust began to settle, the full extent of the disarray in the henhouse became visible.

The floor lay littered with feathers and hay strewn about everywhere. Shattered eggs, dripping with yolk, could be found on virtually every surface; a result of the egg grenades that had been launched during the attack. It was as if a cyclone had touched down and repeatedly spun its rage. The enclosure was in total shambles. Farmer Johnston would lose his marbles when he saw it.

*   *   *

In the Rooster Club, the mood was far more jovial. All the boys were gathered together for a good, old fashioned, cockfight. A makeshift octagon had been quickly constructed out of old pallets and chicken fencing and the excitement mounted as the two fighters prepared to do battle.

"The rules are very simple boys," Rick declared to the anxiously awaiting crowd. "These two warriors will continue kicking and biting until one of the three Dees occurs."

He threw a wing up in the air and held out a feather as he began to explain. "Dee-one. Death. You die, you lose the fight."

Holding up a second feather he continued, "Dee-two. Dismemberment. Lose a body part, you lose the fight."

Finally, up came the third feather. "Dee-three. Dishonour. If you quit, you not only lose the fight but also your sense of honour," he snarled. "Any rooster choosing the third option will be immediately placed on work detail for an undisclosed period of time. We have to sell 'tough' to the other coops. Quitting isn't tough. Quitting is for sissies. Our audience wants violent endings, not cowardly finishes. Personally I'd rather die, or lose a foot, than quit."

Turning to the two combatants, Rick gave Marty and Craig one last chance to bow out. "Any second thoughts?" he asked, "or do you brave beasts think you can handle the conditions as they have been set?" Without even a pause to consider their options both fighters nodded their heads, still raring to go. The cameras were rolling and kibble had been anted up. All that remained was Rick's final word.

"All right you two gladiators," Rick announced. "On my cluck, start pecking!" Marty, the young cockerel, stepped across the ring from Craig. The hulking Delaware was already in his corner taking practice swipes through the air. The two stood and stared, sizing each other up. Finally, Rick gave the highly anticipated chirp. The fight was on.

Craig grossly outweighed his smaller counterpart by an easy seven pounds and the crowd sensed a quick and nasty demise for young Marty. After a few faked shots, the Delaware took the first poke, swinging a haymaker at the smaller combatant. The tiny cockerel quickly dodged to his right, avoiding the blow, coming back at Craig with a kick to the shin. Squawking in pain, Craig reached out to grab Marty but the youngster once again dodged out of the way. With the Delaware out of position, and open to attack, Marty made his move. Like a lightning bolt he opened his beak and charged, grabbing hold of Craig's left wattle. As he bit down with all his might, the Delaware squealed, and recoiled in agony, dropping like a lead balloon.

A nervous murmur rose from the audience as they saw that Marty had taken control of the fight. *All* of the spectators had bet on the Delaware thus there was plenty of kibble on the line to be lost. At the moment, the big rooster was getting his comb handed to him by the little sprite. The crowd quickly rallied to support the fallen scrapper.

"C'mon man, get up and destroy that little elf! You can do it!"

"You're not going to lose to that little pipsqueak, are you?"

"Stand up man. Bite him back! Slap him in the beak! Kick him in the keel! Sit on him! For the love of Mother-Cluck, do something!"

In spite of the encouragement, the Delaware remained on the ground, reeling in pain, his wattle throbbing. Sensing the opportunity to put away his prey, the young cockerel spread his wings wide, took two steps back, and charged. A collective groan rose from the throng of spectators. Marty was pulling the 'ancient eye-peck maneuver'; the oldest trick in the book. Craig was finished, and every-fowl knew it. It took one good jab to eyeball with a ferocious head butt for him to choose his 'Dee'. Shrieking in agony, he raised his wing high, signaling 'Dishonour'. The fight was over.

Another groan rose from the audience. The fight was officially over. Rick took one look at the Delaware writhing in agony, and flashed an unnerving little grin. Every-fowl in the crowd had bet on Craig, meaning Rick had just earned himself a mother load of kibble. "Sorry boys," he announced to the onlookers. "Looks like the house takes home the pot tonight."

Betting slips were slammed to the ground and cusses could be heard throughout the Rooster Club. Rick allowed the discourse to continue for a moment before readdressing the angry mob. He made a motion with his wing for the camera to be turned off. "Tomorrow night, same time, same place," he announced joyfully. "Two more of you will need to volunteer to be the main event."

The roosters all looked at each other nervously. After what they had just witnessed, enthusiasm for being the featured fighters had waned considerably. The moaning Delaware, who still lay writhing in pain, bleeding from the eyeball, had taken most of the glamour out of being a participant.

"We'll need to know who's scrapping by the noon feed so we can get word out to the other barns," Rick demanded.

"Another rule of business; in order to sell it, we need to advertise and promote it."

Turning to the oversized Delaware Rick cast an icy glare, "I'll see you right after the morning wake up call, you sorry excuse for a rooster! If you think you're in pain now, just wait until you see what tomorrow brings, you gizzardless coward." Craig lifted his head and stared up at Rick for a moment with his non-bleeding eye before crumpling back to the dirt.

"Let this be a message to you all," he pronounced to the rest of the brood. "This oversized reject is a disgrace to our species. If we are going to sell our product we have to make it worth buying. Does every-fowl here understand what I'm saying?" The roosters all nodded. They understood Rick perfectly. Quitting was no longer a viable option. Secretly they all hoped Rick would forget about the fights by morning.

As the boys dispersed back to their stalls, Rick beckoned to Marty who was still basking in the glory of victory. Rick gently placed his wing around the smaller rooster's saddle. "Do you always fight like that Marty?" he inquired curiously. "Are you always so tenacious in your attack?"

Marty looked up at Rick and couldn't help but grin; pleased his efforts in the ring had caught the leader's attention. "Yes sir. I always put one hundred and ten percent into everything I do."

Rick nodded and smiled back. "Good Marty. That's good to hear." Reaching under his wing he pulled out a cigarette and offered it to the young scrapper, who readily placed it in his beak. "Tomorrow I am going to have to kick old Dirk Stevens out of this coop along with his chip-chomping brother and that other prudish little hen. It would be helpful to have a little extra muscle, you know, to ensure the deportation goes smoothly. I'd like *you* to be that muscle Marty, to serve as my main wingman. What do you say? Are you in?"

Marty looked up at Rick, his face beaming. "Am I in? Are you kidding me? You don't have to ask me that question twice," he replied proudly. "Darn right I'll be your wingman. It'll be an honour to serve with you sir."

"Excellent," Rick answered, rubbing his wings together. "Our prisoners will be collected tomorrow, right before the noon feed. Once those imbeciles have been permanently removed from the premises, I will have total control of how business is conducted in this coop. And *you* Marty, shall be right by my side."

"You won't be sorry you chose me for this role," Marty exclaimed happily. "I'll be the best wingman ever!"

"I have no doubt you will," Rick agreed, lighting up a cigarette. "Now run along and get some rest, tomorrow is going to be an historical day."

Nine

Morning light came and the three captives welcomed their final day in the coop with a series of grunts and groans. The night had been less than spectacular for Dirk, Derek and Sandra, not one of them catching a wink of sleep. Dirk spent the night sprawled out on a hay bale, fraught with worry. Worry at what was going on in the coop. *His* coop. Dejectedly, he realized that he had been unable to hold things together. He had failed his kin, much like his brother always predicted he would.

If only I had stepped in right away when Rick disrespected me, he thought sadly. *None of this would have happened.*

In addition to being an emotional mess, Dirk was also overcome with confusion. The sun was up, it was twenty after six, and Rick had yet to sound the wake-up call. The hums of snoring barnyard animals cut through the calm of the morning. Farmer Johnston would not be happy! This was his day to go to the market and the chickens were expected to be both awake *and* working hard when he came to collect his eggs.

As it was, Farmer Johnston was already agitated as he made his way out to the chicken coop. His guts still gurgled from terrible stomach cramps that had kept him awake most of the night. He vowed it would be the last time he'd ever eat his wife's beef enchiladas. His morning mission was to feed the chickens and collect the eggs as quickly as possible. If he was speedy there'd be just enough time for a quick nap after breakfast before he headed out to the market.

Tired, and grumpy, the farmer arrived at the food trough with a big bag of fresh corn niblets. *That's weird*, he thought to himself. *Usually the little fellas are out here fighting for position. There's not a fowl to be seen. Where can they all be?* The immediate response that flashed through his mind was cause for grave concern. Coyotes!

Every now and then a coyote or two found its way into the coop. Usually this led to a negative experience for the hapless chickens. The last time a coyote stopped by, the henhouse ended up looking like a scene out of a bad horror flick. It had taken the farmer a week to clean up all the half-eaten carcasses that had been graciously left behind. Farmer Johnston dropped the bag of grub and took off in a sprint towards the henhouse, petrified at what he would find. His poor chickens!

Instead of death and destruction, Farmer Johnston was met with, well, just destruction. His jaw dropped to the floor as his brain processed the sight before him. What a spectacle it was. Eggs were smeared against the walls and stray feathers littered the floor. Hay was scattered throughout the hut, as were pieces of broken nests and crinkled notes that had once been posted on Face-Beak walls. Not a single hen stirred as the farmer wandered through the enclosure in hopes of finding an unbroken egg or two. All the ladies were still recovering from the dance and ensuing riot.

"Stupid hens," he muttered under his breath. "I don't have a single egg to take to the market." He spat out a slew of obscenities and stormed towards the door. *What a bunch of selfish little cluckers. They're all going to have a little visit from my leather belt when I get home tonight.* As he slammed the door to the henhouse not a single occupant stirred from her sleep. Not one.

The farmer's next stop was the Rooster Club, where the picture didn't get any prettier. Stumbling upon the roosters, passed out in their stalls, his frustration continued to mount. On the ground next to one of the stalls, something caught his eye. "Is this a cigarette?" he exclaimed in amazement to no one in particular. *A cigarette in a non-smoking coop? I must be hallucinating.*

He reached over to pick up the half smoked stick when a wing shot out and grabbed hold of his hand with a vice-like grip. Rick stared straight up at the farmer with a look so chilled it would have frozen the Hawaiian lava beds. Carefully removing the cigarette from Farmer Johnston's hand, he placed it back in his beak, curled up in his nest, and returned to his peaceful slumber.

Farmer Johnston stared at the rooster for a moment before shaking his head. "I don't have time for this," he complained, as his guts gave another unsettling gurgle. "I have to be at the market by noon. You all will pay the price for this when I get back!" he announced angrily to the sleeping roosters.

It wasn't until nine o'clock that Rick finally opened his eyes again. He stretched out one mighty wing and then the other before standing up and giving himself a shake. Letting out a long and graceful toot, he expunged the gas that had built up in his gullet overnight. Elegantly lighting up his half smoked cigarette he strutted out across the yard to his new perch. It was finally time to address his subordinates for the first time as their leader. Standing on the fencepost he squawked out a scratchy rendition of, "Cockle-Doodle-Doo!"

Standing and smoking on the fencepost, he waited patiently as the chickens stirred from their roosts and headed out into the yard to join him. "I hope you all enjoyed the extra sleep this morning," he announced with a grin when all were finally present. "Nothing like a few extra winks to start the day."

"What time *is* it?" a young hen asked, using a wing to rub the sleep from her eyes.

Rick smiled at her. "It's just a little past nine," he replied. "A perfect time to get this show moving."

The chickens all looked back and forth at one another in alarm. "How will we get all our work done?" asked one of the roosters. "We're up three hours later than usual."

Rick glared at the little supplicant like he'd just taken a dump in the water trough. "Starting today, work is secondary; secondary to having fun. If you don't get all your work done, it means you had too much to do in the first place. Farmer Johnston will have to get it into his big, fat, head that we aren't going to be bossed around the yard anymore. Not while I am in command!"

Again the chickens looked around at one another. Many began to feel a sudden sense of unease. If they didn't do their work, the farmer wouldn't need them anymore. If he didn't need them anymore, they would be shipped off for processing.

"This is my coop now!" Rick continued. "I make the rules, I make the hours, and I give the orders." Both Darryl and Dwayne clucked their support, but Rick took notice of the many bewildered gazes being directed towards him. He realized that his troops needed some calming words of reassurance.

"Listen folks, I know this is a big adjustment for most of you, but, I need you all to look at the big picture. You'll still get the work done; only now it will be on *your* schedule. Farmer Johnston will still get what he needs from you, and you'll still get what you need from him. It'll just take our dear farmer a few days to recognize that *his* schedule will need some adjustment."

Rick's words seemed to sooth and relax the roosters. It made perfect sense. Farmer Johnston wouldn't care *when* the work was done. So long as it *was* done, he would be content. Once Rick was convinced the chickens were seeing things his way, he launched into his next pitch.

"I would now like to introduce you all to the concept of morning activities!" he exclaimed to the group.

"What are morning activities?" Marty chirped inquisitively.

"I'm glad you asked Marty," Rick replied, giving his wingman a quick wink and a nod. "Instead of the silly things you used to *have* to do, you'll now get to take part in something you actually *want* to do."

"Like what Rick?" Dwayne chirped. "What will we be doing?"

"Well," Rick answered, "a lot of you roosters are looking a little soft. I thought maybe I'd toughen you up a bit today by introducing you to the fine art of body ink?"

The roosters all cocked their heads in unison, "What's body ink?" Darryl asked.

Rick chuckled, "Tattoos boys. I'm going to give you all a tattoo." The roosters all clucked with excitement as their heads bobbed up and down. No fowl in the coop had ever seen a tattoo until Rick showed up. He had lots and they made him look awesome. There was nothing like a nasty picture on the wing to make a bird tougher. Soon all the roosters would be cool and tough like Rick and that made them very happy.

"I will also be selling smokes down at the Rooster Club," he continued with a smile. "Any rooster or hen who has the want, or feels the need to light up, come on down and see me with three pieces of kibble. This ain't a no smoking coop any longer. Farmer Johnston can take that rule and blow it out his old wazoo. You want a cigarette, smoke away."

The chickens all cheered. Now they could smoke. Were they ever lucky. What a great leader Rick was turning out to be. Tattoos, fights, cheap cigarettes and no early morning work; could the coop get any better?

"What'll *we* do Rick, while the boys are getting tattooed?" Janet asked curiously, sticking out her chest and sucking in her saddle.

"Ladies," Rick announced, turning on the charm, "I need you to all go and doll yourselves up like you've never dolled yourselves up before! I'm getting a little lonely and feel the need for some female companionship. So, we're going to have a little competition, kind of like a pageant." Rick gave the gals a knowing little wink and nod.

A companion? Had they heard him correctly? That could only mean one thing. Rick was looking for the future Mrs. Rick. "Go on," he encouraged. "All of you! I need you looking your finest by the noon feed. I want you to make my selection process very difficult," he added with a creepy little squawk. Before Rick had even finished speaking, the hens were running at top speed back to the henhouse in a lust-filled, estrogen-fueled frenzy. Today was the day they had been waiting for. The day that one lucky girl would become Rick's official lady! Not a single hen wanted to miss the opportunity to take home that honour.

As the ladies stampeded away, Rick turned to the boys. "Alright fellas, now that they're gone, let's get back to the Rooster Club. It's tattoo time!"

The roosters all clucked excitedly at the thought of looking mean like Rick. Times in the coop were awesome. They had been right to elect Rick as their leader. He had a plan and a vision that was quickly making life way more enjoyable. What would he come up with next? With an ace like Rick leading the charge, the possibilities were endless!

*   *   *

The High Jinx Meter in the henhouse was still stuck on red as the hen drama picked up where it had left off the night before. Neither Janet, nor Gladys had any mind to let up on one another. "Hey dog-face! I hope you don't drown in tears today when Rick chooses me as his gal," Janet squawked at her former BFF.

"Don't be so sure of yourself, horse-mouth," Gladys shot back. "I'm pretty sure Rick's idea of the perfect hen excludes one that looks like the farmer just drove the rototiller over her face."

"At least I don't have to fluff out my feathers to make my keel look bigger," Janet boasted. "My big keel is natural."

"You're dead!" Gladys roared, clenching both wings in preparation of a strike.

"Whoa there skunk-breath," Janet chuckled, holding her wing out like a stop sign. "Save your energy, ugly. This little spat will resolve itself at the noon feed, when Rick chooses his official lady."

Gladys nodded and flashed an insincere smile, "Bring it on buzzard-beak. And don't forget your crying towel. You'll need it to mop up your tears of rejection when it's *me* Rick chooses as his number one."

* * *

The Rooster Club was hopping as final preparations were made for the tattoo parlour to open. The roosters were incontinent with excitement as they stood, smoking and chatting, awaiting their new ink. Well, almost every rooster was excited.

Craig's morning had been less than spectacular with little hope for improvement. Following the morning sound off, Rick had pulled him aside and laid out his daily duties, one of which was to clean the entire Rooster Club from floor to ceiling. "Be sure to get every nook and cranny you big sissy," Rick had demanded with a scowl. "If you run out of cleaning supplies you'll have to use your mouth and lick up the rest of the mess. I suggest you start with the washrooms while materials are still abundant." Humiliated,

Craig continued scrubbing, avoiding contact with the other fowl. As they laughed and smoked, he miserably worked at completing his unpleasant chores.

"I think I want a skull with flames," Darryl declared, sitting down next to Rick as he pulled out his tattoo needles. "A big skull with burning flames."

"That will make you look so tough," Dwayne chirped. "I think I am going to go with a rusty anchor that has a poisonous snake wrapped around it."

Rick nodded in agreement as he continued digging out his equipment. "Nice choices boys, you should look nice and tough when I'm done with you," he remarked. "Alright Darryl, sit down and hold still, this may pinch a bit at first."

As the needle dug into Darryl's wing it did more than just pinch a bit. It hurt like a son of a hen. The pain was worse than the time he had caught his left wattle in the bathroom door. Half squawking, half screaming, he let out a window shattering, guttural belch that shook the Rooster Club on its foundation. "Owwwww! It hurts, it hurts, please stop! PLEASE STOP!"

Rick looked at him, and slowly removed the needle. His expression changed from one of indifference to one of complete disgust. He carefully reached into his equipment bag and pulled out an old sweat sock, which he promptly shoved into Darryl's gaping beak.

"Bite down on that, you sissy," he exclaimed impatiently holding the needle up to Darryl's face. "You squawk like that again and I'll jab you in the eyeball with this thing." Darryl's eyes grew the size of saucers and he instantly clammed up, too frightened to mutter another peep. Seeing his message had been received, Rick casually returned to his art work.

When the skull and flames were finally etched into Darryl's wing, he stood up and triumphantly displayed his new ink. The other roosters clucked their approval at his new tat. "Looks good man," one shouted out. "Can't wait to get mine!"

Rick reached under his wing and pulled out another cigarette. "Yeah, about that. I'm kinda pooped fellas," he admitted, lighting his poison stick. "Being a leader really takes a lot out of a guy." The others had to agree. Rick had been very busy since taking over the reigns of leadership. "I'm going to head back to my stall for a little nap before lunch. Noon feed is going to be pretty busy with the banishment and all. We can finish the tattoos tomorrow if that's okay."

The roosters all responded in support of Rick. Of course it was okay if he finished tomorrow. They needed their leader well rested to make good decisions on their behalf. A nap sounded like the perfect idea.

"While I'm resting, you lads can figure out who's scrapping tonight? There's a stag party at Farmer Patterson's tomorrow and they want to watch a good fight. The boys down there will pay big kibble for one of our recordings, so this one needs to be a dandy. A *real* fight to the death!" The roosters looked around at one another other nervously. None of them wanted to end up like Craig, licking the toilets, or even worse, *dead.*

"Think it over boys, talk it out. I want to announce the main event today at the noon feed. Maybe even invite the hens to come watch. The more the merrier! In the meantime I'm heading back to my nest. Don't disturb me for any reason. I need my beauty sleep."

Rick turned and started to waddle back to his lair. As an afterthought he wheeled around and barked out a final order to Craig, "Take some scraps down to our pathetic little prisoners. Let them know this is officially their last meal in the coop. As of noon, those cluckers are out of here!"

Ten

As the morning wore on, tensions began to rise between the Stevens brothers as they started getting restless in the lock-up. "If you would have just dealt with the situation when he first got here, none of this would have happened!" Derek shouted angrily at his brother. "You'd still be in charge, and we'd all be free."

"What did you want me to do Derek? I thought he would come around after a little relocation anxiety," Dirk replied defensively.

"Well, you thought wrong little brother." Derek pointed out, stating the obvious. "Now we're stuck in this filthy, roach infested hole, while that tattooed sociopath plans for our deportation."

"Well, I didn't see you do anything to stop him either Derek," Dirk shot back. "You let him manipulate and steal your two best friends. Then you came running to me to bail you out."

"Ya, well, I guess I thought that as leader you had the power to do something about it. Guess I was wrong!"

"Stop!" Sandra hissed. "Both of you!" She had heard enough banter from the Stevens boys. "If you two think arguing and blaming one another is going to get us out of this mess, then we're all finished. The only way we're going to get out of this jam is if we all work together!"

Dirk glanced over at Sandra, then back at Derek before nodding. "She's right bro," he agreed. "We are the only hope this coop has at survival. You and I are going to have to put aside our differences for the time being and work together. If that filthy louse remains in power much longer, our barnyard is going to self-destruct."

Begrudgingly Derek nodded his head in agreement. "But what are we going to do? Realistically, what *can* we do? There is a whole slew of them, and only three of us. All our fellow fowl are living under Rick's spell right now. They are holding him in higher regard than dear old Mother-Cluck. We're fighting a battle we have no chance at winning."

The three stood silent for a moment. As thoughts of despair flew through Derek's mind, it came to him. A solution. A solution that would save his kin from Rick's evil clutches. His eyes grew as large as basketballs and his belly quivered uncontrollably. "If you want to kill a chicken, you cut off its head!" he announced, throwing a wing in the air triumphantly. "And that's exactly what we have to do."

Dirk looked at his brother in wonder and shook his head. "We can't kill them Derek," he replied. "We aren't murderers."

"I'm not talking about murder you simpleton" he shot back. "That was just a metaphor. I'm talking about cutting off the head, as in the head of the group. Our good buddy Rick."

Dirk gazed at his brother, confused, before turning to Sandra, "Do you have any idea what the heck he's talking about?" he asked, voice full of exasperation.

Sandra slowly nodded. "Yes, believe it or not, I think I do. And, what's more, it makes perfect sense. What he's saying is, in order to conquer the whole group, we must first take down the leader."

"Exactly!" Derek chirped excitedly. "That's exactly what I was saying. Which means, if we are going to save this coop, all we have to do is take down Rick!" Derek finished by slapping his brother on the saddle. "It's as easy as that. If Rick goes down, the rest of the fowl will revert back to their normal selves. They won't feel that their purpose in life is to impress him. End of problems, coop saved!"

All three stood silently for what seemed like an eternity before Dirk finally tabled the question they had all been pondering. "So, how, are we going to go about taking down Rick?"

Sandra looked at her feet and Derek shrugged. "I don't know," Derek replied, "but I'm out of chips, and I need chips to think straight. Besides, I came up with the *idea* in the first place. The *plan* is your responsibility. I can't do everything you know."

As the prisoners stood around considering their options, Craig came meandering along with a bucket of slop. The three couldn't help but notice the black eye he was sporting. "Here's some gruel for you folks," he said, without emotion, dumping the bucket of mush through the chicken fence. "Rick says it's all you're getting until your banishment, so ration it wisely."

"What! That's our meal?" Derek squawked angrily. "I wouldn't feed that crap to a swan! Where are my chips?"

Craig stared back at Derek blankly and shrugged his wings. "Dude, I'm just doing what I'm told. Don't shoot the messenger. If you don't like it, don't eat it."

"I'd rather eat my own offspring," Derek retorted.

Craig shrugged, "Suit yourself then. I'm just the delivery boy. I could care less if you eat it or not."

Dirk carefully inspected the wounded Delaware. "Buddy," he said with concern in his voice. "Your face looks like it got run over by an aerator. Are you okay?"

The Delaware looked down at his feet in shame. "Ya, I'm okay," he replied.

"You sure don't look okay," Dirk continued. "Look at your wattle? It's the size of a tennis ball."

The big Delaware looked back at Dirk sadly, "Forget it, it's nothing," he said. "I got a little carried away at the dance last night and fell at the water trough. Whacked myself up pretty good, eh? The swelling should go down in a day or two."

"No you didn't," Dirk accused. "There's no way you could mangle a wattle that badly by going for a drink of water. No way at all."

"Well, whatever," the Delaware replied, turning to leave, tears beginning to well in his eyes. "Just forget it, it's nothing. I have to get back to the Rooster Club so I can finish cleaning out the stalls."

"I bet you were in one of Rick's staged fights weren't you?" Derek blurted out, pointing a wing at Craig. "I know all about those fights. I lost my two best friends because of them. Rick is just using all you roosters for his own personal gain."

"I don't know what you're talking about," Craig replied curtly. "I already told you, I tripped at the water trough. End of story. I have to go."

"What's your name?" Sandra asked calmly, her quiet tone softening the Delaware's hard stance.

Slightly taken aback by the softness in her voice, the large Delaware sheepishly replied, "Craig. My name is Craig."

"Craig, we can help you," Dirk offered, a plan coming together in his head. "But to help you, we need you to help us."

Eyes watering, Craig shook his head. "I can't let you go," he explained sadly. "Rick would rip my wings off."

"No, no," Dirk replied shaking his head and holding his wings out in a calming motion. "I'm not asking you to let us go. I just need you to share a little information with me."

Craig looked over his shoulders nervously, checking to ensure he was alone. He put his head up against the wires of the enclosure and lowered his voice to a whisper, "I can't. Like I already told you, Rick will limb me if I don't get back to the Rooster Club right now."

"Newsflash Craig," Dirk shot back. "If something doesn't happen, and happen quickly, you'll all be sent out and processed anyway. Farmer Johnston doesn't need a bunch of chickens that sleep in all morning and party all night. He needs chickens that are going to lay eggs and take care of business. Failure to do so will lead to all of you being sold and slaughtered."

Craig considered his moral dilemma. Any way he looked at it, he was up the creek without a paddle. Dirk was right. The minute the chickens stopped producing for Farmer Johnston they were as good as dead. However, as soon as he crossed Rick, he was also as good as dead. It was a lose/lose situation for poor old Craig. He had to determine the option that presented him with the best chance for survival.

After a speedy soul search, Craig made his decision. "What do you need me to do?"

Dirk smiled and motioned for Craig to come closer. "Tell me what's been going on big fella. Tell me every dirty detail."

Nervously, Craig recounted the comings and goings of the coop. He spoke of the drama-filled henhouse; the ruthless cockfighting, dancing the night away, tattoo parlours, and the oversleeping. Dirk, Derek and Sandra all listened intently. "Basically, the High Jinx Meter is redder than Farmer Johnston's beets, the roosters are on testosterone overload and Rick is sitting back enjoying the chaos. Anarchy has completely taken over!"

There was a moment of silence as the stream of information was carefully processed. Finally Dirk spoke up. "What are his plans for us?"

Craig looked around again; making sure no fowl was within earshot. "He is banishing you from the barnyard, permanently, today at the noon feed."

Both Sandra and Derek gasped, but Dirk grinned, undeterred. "So he is parading us out in front of an audience?" he asked.

"Yes," Craig replied sheepishly. "He wants to shame you in front of the entire brood before giving you the boot. Every chicken on the farm will be there."

The grin on Dirk's beak turned into a full-blown smile. "Excellent!" he remarked happily.

"Excellent?" Derek blurted out ferociously. "Are you on crack? He's threatening us with banishment and public shame, and you react with a giggle and a grin? What is wrong with you?"

Dirk continued smiling, ignoring his ranting brother. "By the time evening feed rolls around *we* will be back in our own stalls and *I* will be Mr. Stevens once again," he announced cheerfully. "By tonight Rick will be nothing more than a fading memory."

"And how do you plan on accomplishing this?" Derek asked, unconvinced.

Dirk, once again ignoring his brother's lack of faith, turned to the big Delaware. "Craig, this is what we need you to do."

Eleven

Craig returned to the Rooster Club and continued cleaning the stalls as per Rick's instructions. His little chat with Dirk had provided a shimmer of hope that his torment would soon be over. Many of his fellow fowl were napping, still exhausted from the dance. Those that weren't asleep were engaged in other quiet activities. Two sat up smoking and playing cards, while a few others sprawled out quietly in a corner, smoking and discussing tattoo possibilities.

None of them even gave Craig a second glance. As far as they were concerned he was a rung below donkey manure on the ladder of life.

Checking around to ensure some of the boys were within earshot, Craig began to mumble to himself. Hearing him, the card-playing roosters stopped their game and looked over in his direction. "Are you talking, wimp?" one called out. "I'm pretty sure that would make Rick very unhappy. Can't very well lick our stalls clean if you're busy yapping."

Craig glanced back at them. "Sorry fellas, I must have been mumbling about the **big fight** without even knowing it. I'll stop talking to myself about the **big fight**. My apologies for mentioning the **big fight**. I'll get back to work and you can forget I ever said anything about the **big fight**. Sorry."

The two roosters laid down their cards and stared at Craig curiously. Slowly they stood up from the overturned crate they were using as a table and waddled over to where the large Delaware continued scrubbing. "What big fight?" one questioned, a cigarette dangling loosely from his beak. "Last I heard, we ain't chose no fighters for tonight."

"Ya," added the other. "What big fight are you talking about?"

Craig, looked around cautiously, then softly whispered his reply. "It's kind of a secret but I overheard Rick talking about it with one of the other roosters. He and Dirk Stevens are going to go beak to beak at the noon feed," he revealed. "Rumour has it, they are going to fight to the death."

"What?" one bellowed out loud. "Dirk and Rick? Rick will kill him!"

"Awesome!" declared the other. "I can't wait to see Rick tear Dirk's head off and wear it like a hat!"

Craig quickly held the tip of his wing up to his beak in an attempt to quiet the two twits. "Shhhh," he cautioned. "Can't let too many chickens know about this. I'm sure Dirk is a little worried that a big crowd will show up and watch him get destroyed. The smaller the audience, the less humiliating it will be for him."

The two looked at one another and squawked. "Are you kidding? No way are we keeping this quiet. I'm telling every single chicken I see. All the fowl in this coop have the right to know when a good old-fashioned tail kicking is gonna take place. In fact, I'm going to post this on all the Face-Beak stall walls right now."

"Yeah," agreed the other. "This is going to be awesome. Dirk is gonna die, and we're gonna get to watch! C'mon, let's go spread the word."

Craig kept a straight face, but was chuckling on the inside as the two roosters dashed away at top speed to share the exciting news. The seed had been planted and the weed was already beginning to grow. Satisfied, Craig returned to his cleaning duties. Dirk's plan had been set in motion. *Flawlessly,* he thought to himself with a shimmer of pride. Everything had happened exactly as predicted. Sighing happily, he realized that life in the barnyard would soon be returning to normal.

* * *

The hens were about three quarters of the way through dolling themselves up when news of the big battle broke: Rick vs. Dirk, high noon, at the water trough. Of course the story had changed a little as it generally does when passed down from chicken to chicken. The latest version of the tale had Rick publicly executing Dirk with his bare wings, then feeding on his carcass while it made its last few twitches.

"This is wonderful! Rick is going to finally demonstrate his true strength. I will make sure I'm right there beside him as he steals Dirk's last breath," Gladys boasted.

"That makes sense," Janet replied smiling. "He can use your horrible smell to knock Dirk out without having to break a sweat." A wave of giggles passed through Janet's friends as Gladys' wattles turned three different shades of red. "Then he can expend all that extra energy on a little 'behind the barn' time with me!"

"Keep dreaming," Gladys squawked angrily. "The only extra energy he'll be wasting on you is the energy it takes to cover his eyes and run."

The bickering continued as Janet and Gladys exchanged a new batch of offensive insults. However, aside from their unrelenting animosity, an absolute certainty had developed: Every hen in the coop would be watching as handsome Rick squared off against Dirk Stevens. Every hen would be on the sidelines, cheering on their leather-clad leader, in hopes of becoming the future love of his life.

*   *   *

As word of the fight spread through the Rooster Club there was a shared sense of both excitement and relief. The boys were all excited about the heavyweight scrap between the present and former leaders. They were also relieved that it wouldn't be any of *them* stepping into the ring. If Rick and Dirk were squaring off, it meant they weren't. All would live to cluck another day.

From his nest, Rick began to stir from his nap. Slowly standing to work out the grogginess, and a little excess gas, he caught bits and pieces of the roosters' conversation. *"Rick, Dirk, fight, noon."* Instantly his eyes popped open and the haziness disappeared.

Rick waddled out into the common area to join the excited roosters. "Tear him a new one Rick," Dwayne encouraged, noticing the mighty leader was once again gracing them with his presence.

"Ya man, destroy that loser! Make him scream for mercy, then rip his beak off!" Darryl added, handing Rick a cigarette.

Lighting up, Rick stared at the group and smiled. "It won't be pretty boys," he replied calmly, no clue as to what they were actually talking about. "I hope he has a good life insurance policy. His family is gonna need it."

Scouring the crowd, he locked eyes with Marty. "Marty," he beckoned with his wing. "Come for a little walk with me."

Marty obediently followed Rick into the yard. Once out of sight, and earshot of the others, Rick grabbed the little cockerel by the throat and pulled his face up close to his own. "Marty, what the cluck are those guys talking about in there?" he asked, anger masking his concern.

Marty shrugged. "Huh? What do you mean? It's trending all over the barnyard. You know? The big fight. You and Dirk squaring off at the noon feed? Rumour has it you're planning on roasting his corpse after you win."

Rick slowly released his tight grip on Marty's neck and stood down. "Yeah," he chuckled, a hint of uneasiness detectable in his tone. "That's about right. Guess my little secret is out. I was trying to keep it a surprise," Rick lied coolly. "Who told you anyway?"

Again, Marty shrugged. "I'm not too sure really. I heard it from a lot of places. Like I said, it's the only topic of conversation around here right now. I think I heard first from Darryl, who I think got it from Dwayne who I think heard it from a couple of guys who were playing cards that claim they found out from Craig."

Rick processed the flow of information and came to a speedy conclusion. *Craig. That blasted Delaware.* He had taken the food down to the pen and conjured up something with that reject, Dirk Stevens. What were they planning?

Rick was damned if he did and damned if he didn't. If he didn't fight, he'd look like a sissy and lose all credibility. However, if he did fight, there was a really good chance he'd get his comb bashed in. Rick was a number of things, a good fighter not being one of them. His intimidating nature, and rough appearance generally kept him from having to throw the wings around.

"I can't wait to see you drop that lame piece of grit," Marty exclaimed. "This place is way better now that you're in charge."

"Well, it should be a short scrap," Rick agreed, an idea beginning to form in his tiny little noggin. "Even if my right wing *was* injured last week in a rumble down at Farmer Beaton's."

"Wow!" Marty interrupted, sucked in by Rick's tale. "You were in a rumble? That's so awesome."

"Yeah, well," Rick replied nonchalantly with a shrug. "I've been in plenty of brawls. I find they help pass the time."

"But, if your wing is injured, maybe you shouldn't fight," Marty pointed out instinctively. "Maybe you should keep Dirk and company in lock up until your wing is healed. You know, postpone it a day or two."

"There's no way we're postponing this fight Marty. No way!" Rick replied with a smile, regaining composure by taking a long haul off his cigarette. "To be honest, I'm not all that worried about my wing. In fact, truth be told, I'm pretty sure I could whip Dirk's tail with *two* bad wings. However, to give me a few extra minutes to prepare for the banishment, maybe you could take my place and head down with Darryl and Dwayne to pull our unwanted guests out of lock up."

"Sure," Marty replied eagerly. "I'd love to."

Rick's voice took on an ominous undertone as he stared back at Marty with his cold grey eyes. "And Marty," he added, his tone so sinister it made the young cockerel shudder. "If something were to happen to Dirk during transport, I would understand."

Marty looked up at Rick, confused. "I'm not sure what you mean?"

"It's like this Marty. Let's just say, I would be open to Dirk having a little 'accident' on his way up to the trough," Rick remarked suggestively.

"You mean like him getting his tail feathers caught in the gate or something like that?" Marty asked, still not picking up the hidden meaning in Rick's message.

"No Marty, I mean like him accidentally being beaten to death by you," Rick squawked in exasperation. Quickly maintaining his poise, he flashed a little wink and nod at Marty. The young cockerel nodded back, Rick's message now crystal clear.

Twelve

Farmer Johnston left a few piles of kibble beside the water trough before leaving for the market. He had been tempted to starve his moronic chickens but Mrs. Johnston had talked him out of it. "Skinny chickens lay sickly little eggs," she insisted. Still incensed, he planned on giving them all a piece of his mind, and his belt when he returned home that evening. Angrily he sped away in his pick-up, with little more than a few of his wife's fresh bunt cakes to sell.

At roughly the same time the farmer was tearing off down the lane, Dwayne, Darryl and Marty were arriving at the lock-up. "We've been sent for the prisoners," Darryl announced taking a long haul off a freshly lit smoke.

"Where's Rick?" Dirk asked. "He too scared to come fetch us himself?"

"Scared? That's a good one," Darryl chirped. "He's busy."

"He's busy? Doing what? Counting all the kibble he won from you losers?" Derek roared furiously. "If you think I'm going anywhere with you two backstabbing sons of hens, you can kiss my feathered . . ."

"Tsk, tsk," Dwayne interrupted with a snicker as he unlocked the pen. "Such language is not very becoming of a young rooster; especially one who is about to be banished forever. What kind of a lasting legacy will that leave?"

Derek stared back at his former BFF with a look of pure hatred. "Don't look so shocked Derek," Dwayne clucked condescendingly. "You had the opportunity to join in on the fun but you chose to be a loser."

"Eat spit!" Derek retorted. "I'd rather chew my own wattles than waste one second smoking and fighting with you two hemorrhoids."

"Shut your beaks!" Marty chirped impatiently. "I'd love to stand here and cluck all day but Rick is waiting. Waiting for *you*," he directed at Dirk, jabbing a pointed wing into the former leader's keel.

Dirk took a step forward and glared into the young cockerel's eyes. "You touch me again and I'll squeeze your throat hard enough to pop those beady eyes right out of your skinny little head."

Dirk's words struck a nerve with the little cockerel who was still feeling larger than life after his big win in the ring. Too naïve, or maybe just too plain stupid to know any better, Marty lunged in anger. Claws wide open, and beak pecking wildly, he threw himself at Dirk, who deftly sidestepped his miniature attacker. Sticking out a wing as Marty passed, Dirk clotheslined the tiny combatant, dropping him to the dirt with a thud. Marty lay stretched out on his back, dazed and winded, wondering how the tables had so quickly been turned. Dirk immobilized the young cockerel by placing his foot directly across Marty's throat.

"All right boys," Dirk directed at Darryl and Dwayne. "You two losers need to get yourselves to the back of this pen. Now!" Dwayne and Darryl looked at one another with stunned expressions, unsure of what to do.

"Maybe you didn't hear me," he repeated. "Either you two nimrods get to the back of this pen, or I will choke this little runt out and then shove you back there myself," Dirk clucked out in anger.

With fear in their eyes Darryl and Dwayne moved to the back of the lock up without incident. Dirk grabbed hold of Marty and tossed him over beside them. The three former captives then stepped out of their prison, Sandra carefully closing and securing the door behind them.

"We'll be back for you once I finish up my business with Rick," Dirk announced with a smile. "There's some left over slop on the ground if you get hungry."

"You won't be going anywhere once Rick is done with you!" Marty shot back angrily, regaining some of his spunk. "You'll be dead! And your two little sidekicks will be banished forever."

"Yeah!" Dwayne and Darryl chirped in unison.

"Really? Is that what you think?" Dirk asked, taking a step back towards the pen. "How do you think Rick is going to respond to the fact that the three of you were overrun by the very prisoners you were sent to retrieve? Based on what *I've* seen, Rick doesn't tolerate failure. I imagine the consequences he puts in place to punish your incompetence won't be very pleasant." Dirk paused for a moment to let the three digest the reality of their situation.

"You all better hope that Rick goes down in this fight. Because, if he doesn't, he'll be coming for you three flops next." Dirk gave a little wave of his wing, leaving the new captives to sit and ponder their futures.

*   *   *

High noon at the water trough was greeted with great anticipation and fanfare. The roosters were all clucks and giggles with excitement. The big fight was moments away and they all wanted a front row seat. The hens arrived in their two separate gaggles, all tarted up to the nines in the quest to become Rick's official dish.

Rick, however, paid no attention to the bickering of the hens or the testosterone overload of the roosters. He was anxiously awaiting word from Marty that Dirk Stevens had been neutralized once and for all. Hiding his edginess by smoking and spitting, he paced back and forth in front of the food trough, praying that his nemesis had been taken out for good.

"Grab some kibble everyone!" he clucked to his supporters. "A slaughter is much more satisfying on a full stomach!"

On Rick's word, the hens and roosters made their way up to the tiny piles of corn niblets and mealworm that had been left out by the farmer. Just as they were about to chow down, a series of angry chirps captured their attention. The crowd parted as Dirk, Derek and Sandra shuffled up, scowls of displeasure on their beaks.

Rick surveyed the situation. Not seeing Marty, Dwayne or Darryl, he came to the quick realization that his little plan had not been carried out as intended. The colour began to drain from his wattles. "What are you losers doing here?" he snapped at the former prisoners, doing his best to mask the anxiety that was slowly taking control of him.

"What are we doing here?" Dirk asked rhetorically. "You're the one who sent for us, remember? You tell me what we're doing here. Word has it you and I have a little score to settle."

Rick stared back at Dirk angrily, cigarette dangling from his beak.

"*And*, how many times do you have to be told," Dirk added, reaching up with his wing and plucking the smoke from Rick's beak, "that this is a non-smoking coop?" Dropping the cigarette to the ground, he stomped it into the dirt. "Why should *my* lungs pay for *your* bad habits?"

A collective gasp of disbelief rose from the on-looking crowd. How would Rick respond to such blatant disrespect? "You're gonna pay for that you little rat-faced spazz," Rick growled shoving Dirk with both wings. "What did you do with my boys?"

"You mean those three incompetent, weasel-nosed castoffs you sent down to fetch us?" Dirk asked with a cheeky grin. "They're back in the lock-up preening one another. If you really want to lead this coop, there is one thing you're going to have to learn."

"And what might that be?" Rick asked with a sneer, tilting his head slightly.

"Never send a cockerel to do a big rooster's job!" Dirk exclaimed triumphantly, driving his forehead into Rick's with enough force to topple the third little pig's house of bricks. The unexpected head-butt dropped Rick to the ground where he momentarily lay dazed and confused. "Now, if I'm not mistaking, you and I have some business to take care of," Dirk confirmed, standing over his fallen foe.

Rick sat up, rubbing his aching head. "Nice cheap shot Stevens. Let's see how you do when I know it's coming."

"In a minute." Dirk replied. "But first, I think we need to lay out some ground rules here."

"How about, no cheap shots," Rick muttered rudely.

Dirk ignored Rick's comments and clucked on, "I have a few rules I think we should follow, you know, to keep this a fair fight."

"I'm the leader around here Stevens, so I make the rules." Rick snarled, picking himself up off the ground. "We fight until *your* death. And when *your* corpse is making its final twitches, your two loser friends will walk their pathetic rumps off this farm forever."

Dirk took a moment to consider the proposal. "Sounds fair enough to me," he agreed calmly. "But, I get to choose the location. I say we head over by the water trough where the ground is level. That will give us both a fair shot at winning."

"Suit yourself," Rick replied with false confidence. "I guess it's only fair that you get choose the location of your own untimely demise."

A large circle of chickens spread out around the trough as the combatants took their positions. Every-fowl chose his or her special spot to stand and enjoy the shake-down. As both roosters squared off, Rick offered Dirk a final opportunity to save face. "Last chance Stevens," he heckled, "forfeit right now, and I'll let you leave this place alive, with at least *some* of your dignity intact."

"Hmmm," Dirk thought for a second, scratching his comb. "Nope. I think I'll take my chances in the ring."

"Enough talk boys, it's time to get this thing on!" a young rooster roared out from the crowd.

"Cockle-Doodle-Kill-Him," shouted another. "Bash his beak in Rick!"

"Rip his wattles off!" cried an elderly hen. "Show him who's boss!"

Rick held a wing up to silence the crowd. Slowly, he removed a cigarette from his jacket pocket, placed it gently in his beak and sparked it up. Then in one fluent motion he swung a surprise roundhouse with his left wing in hopes of catching Dirk off guard.

After years of fighting with his brother, Dirk saw the maneuver coming from a mile away, and deftly side-stepped the telegraphed blow. As Rick's wing followed through, hitting nothing but air, he lost his balance. Seeing his foe stumble, and sensing he was vulnerable, Dirk stepped up and gave him a two-winged chop to the top of the head. Once again Rick crumpled to the ground like a sack of sheep manure.

"You done yet?" Dirk asked politely, standing over his fallen opponent. "Or are you just getting warmed up?"

Rick looked up in a daze, his vision a blur. "Not a chance," he wheezed back stubbornly. "I hope that's not all you've got Stevens!"

Cheers rose from the crowd as Rick staggered to his feet. "Enough with the love taps," he clucked at Dirk. "Time to get serious!"

"Atta boy Rick. Pound him in the gullet!"

"Come on Rick, rip his comb off!"

"Pluck that son of a hen alive Ricky-boy!"

Rick dusted himself off and cast an icy glare at his rival. Dirk glanced back with a big smile. "Ready for round two tough guy?"

"I'm going to rip your head off and shove it up your –." Before Rick could finish his delightful sentiment he found himself in a full wing wrap, being lifted off the ground. Scrambling, he tried to claw his way out of the death grip, but Dirk held on firmly and raised him up over his head. Swiftly he moved towards the trough.

The spectators gasped in horror as Dirk slammed Rick down with a splash, fully submerging him under the water. Flailing his wings, Rick tried to surface, but his attempts to free himself were futile. Dirk's strength was too much for the floundering vigilante.

The thrashing continued as Rick fought for oxygen. With each passing second his efforts at self-preservation grew weaker and weaker. Sensing victory was near; Dirk placed his foot on top of Rick's head, and turned to face the crowd, lifting his wings in triumph.

"What are you doing?" Gladys squawked, fear creeping into her voice. "He can't stay under water like that. You're going to kill him."

Dirk looked over at her, unconcerned, "Yes!" he mocked. "I *am* going to kill him. That's one of the consequences when two roosters fight to the death. One fighter dies. Looks like today, that fighter will be Rick."

"You can't do this," Janet begged. "It isn't right."

"It was his idea," Dirk replied coldly, his voice void of sympathy. "Besides Janet, how dare you stand there and lecture me on doing the right thing? When, in the last two days, has the notion of doing the right thing crossed your simple, little mind? With the way you've been carrying on with Gladys, *please*, spare me the lecture."

It was as Rick gave one final push to save himself that Dirk noticed the coloured filament of scum rising to the water's surface. Curiously he moved in for a closer look. It took a second to register but as he identified the source he let out a belly laugh that echoed throughout the entire barnyard.

"Folks," Dirk clucked at the hushed crowd. "You gotta see this." He grabbed Rick by the comb and yanked him out of the trough. "Take a good look at Mr. Rebel now!"

The chickens all stood and gawked. Something about Rick was certainly different. They couldn't pin point exactly what it was until Dirk pointed it out for them. "Where are your tattoos Rick?"

Rick turned three different shades of green, and not from the oxygen deficiency. His tattoos had disappeared, vanished, washed away in the trough. "Uh, well, they were just, well they were . . ."

"They were fake!" Dirk finished. "You coloured them on with a pen you simple fool. To look tough. They're Fake! Just like this stupid piercing in your comb," Dirk grabbed the ring and yanked it as hard as he could. Rick let out a blood-curdling scream as the flesh of his comb tore open. "Oops," Dirk grimaced, "I guess that one was real. My bad."

"Man, is Darryl ever going to be mad," one rooster whispered to another.

"Tell me about it," came the reply. "The tattoo on *his* wing won't wash off. And, it looks terrible."

The group stared at Rick as he stood, soaked to the bone, with ink running down his feathered body. "It's time to end this thing once and for all," Dirk acknowledged, grabbing hold of his battered foe once again.

"Whoa," Rick replied throwing up a wing. "I surrender. No more. You win. You can stay. Heck, you can even be leader again. Just keep me away from the water. I hate getting wet."

Dirk shook his head with a look of mock sadness on his face. "Sorry Rick, but the deal was that we fight to the death. You were *very* clear on that point. The fact that both of us are still breathing right now tells me that we aren't finished yet." Grasping Rick by the throat Dirk prepared to end things once and for all.

"Stop," a voice said softly from behind the two fighters. Sandra carefully approached the trough and put a wing around Dirk's saddle. "It's over," she repeated. "He's had enough."

One look into her deep blue eyes and Dirk knew she was right. He slowly released his grip on Rick, who collapsed to the ground; grateful his life had been spared.

Dirk scornfully stared down the defeated rebel. "You're getting off easy, you rotten cloaca," he cursed at Rick. "However, your time here is done. You have ten minutes to gather your things and get your sorry tail off this farm," he clucked at his fallen foe. "It's time for you to go back to Farmer Beaton's where you belong!"

Rick's face turned the colour of a polar bear's belly. "No!" he responded forcefully. "There's not a chance that I'm going back there." His voice cracked as he finished his sentence. "I can't go back to Farmer Beaton's," he continued. "The roosters there are mean to me. They treat me like crap, always teasing and tormenting me. That's why I was sent here to begin with. For a fresh start." Rick's beak began to quiver and to the surprise of every-fowl, tears began streaming down his face.

"So you decided to act like a jerk?" Derek squawked angrily, unmoved by Rick's show of emotion. He came out from behind the water trough and approached the blubbering rooster. "Cry all you want. Thanks to *you* my two best friends want nothing to do with me. Thanks to *you* I want nothing to do with them either. I say go back where you came from, you piece of rat fodder! You're not welcome here any more, cry-baby!"

"You don't understand," Rick sobbed. "I can't go back there. It would be a fate worse than death. Please don't make me go. I'll make it up to you all, I promise."

"No mercy! Send him back!" Gladys clucked in agreement. "Thanks to him the henhouse has been a gong show for the past two days."

"Ya," shouted Craig pointing at his black eye and swollen wattles. "I think he's done enough damage here already." Others began joining in, clucking out in support of Rick's banishment. The tide had quickly turned on the former hero.

"Whoa!" Dirk exclaimed, throwing a wing in the air to silence the crowd. "Hold on one minute. Don't any of you dare try and blame Rick for all your troubles. Was he a catalyst? Yes. But, every one of you is responsible for *your* own actions. Rick didn't post any of those nasty messages on your stalls, nor did he force you to try and act cool. You all made those choices for yourselves."

"But he made us fight!" squawked Craig, wattle still throbbing. "Look at my face!"

"Did he really?" Dirk retorted with an exaggerated eye roll. "You mean to tell me that one little cockerel overpowered the entire rooster population of this coop and made them pound the crap out of one another? I don't think so. You did as he asked, not because you had to, but because you wanted to impress him and look cool."

"You know, come to think of it, I think I've changed my mind. Rick stays," Dirk declared. "*And*, Rick's rules are going to remain in effect as well. You voted for them, its time to lie in the bed you've made for yourselves. It's time you all learned to live with the consequences of your actions. Who is fighting tonight anyway? Apparently there's a battle going down on Cockle-Doodle-Doo-Tube. Any volunteers?"

The roosters all looked at one another with alarm. What in the name of Mother-Cluck was Dirk talking about? There was no way any of them wanted to fight. No way at all. "Let's have another vote," Craig piped up. "We can't keep living like this. If all we do is fight and hang out, Farmer Beaton will have us processed."

"Tough," Dirk shot back angrily. "Maybe you should have thought of that yesterday when you so readily voted Rick into power."

All the chickens were fraught with worry. What would they do? Dirk eyed them all for a moment, letting them stew, before finally relenting, "We'll have another vote on one condition," he offered.

"What do we need to do?" a young hen clucked from the crowd. "I can't continue to live under these conditions any longer." The rest of the crowd chirped in agreement. "We have all been very stupid and need to make things right again."

Dirk stared at the brood and considered his options. He felt like choking the life out of each and every one of them, but that would just be a waste of his time and energy. "Your irresponsible actions nearly brought down this coop!" he lectured earnestly. "It makes me sick when I think of how selfish you've all been these past two days." Every head in the yard slowly lowered in shame.

"You hens," he chirped, pointing at the ladies, "will go directly back to the henhouse, clean up the ridiculous mess you've made and take down all your nasty little Face-Beak posts. I want that High Jinx Meter back on green where it belongs. Once your stupid drama has been laid to rest, you can all hop up in your nests and start squeezing out some eggs for the farmer."

Then, directing his anger towards the males, "You meatballs will stop fighting one another," he clucked. "You'll go back and turn the Rooster Club into *our* home again. It will no longer resemble a betting parlour or a boxing ring."

Dirk stopped and looked around at his kin. The roosters nodded, understanding what they needed to do. "When you're done with the Rooster Club, get your sorry combs back out here and clean up the mess from last night's dance. This place looks worse than the pigsty! Farmer Johnston will be back in a couple of hours so there's no time to waste. If he gets back and the barnyard still looks like this, so help me Mother-Cluck. We'll *all* be dead!"

The roosters and hens looked around at one another, heads bobbing. "Alright," Janet finally said, "let's get at it."

"If there are no questions, we will meet at the perch in two hours to decide how to proceed," Dirk announced to his following.

"I have a question," Derek piped up. "What are you going to do with *him*?" he asked in disgust, pointing a wing at Rick.

Dirk laughed out loud. "I have special plans for my little friend," he replied. "A very special set of duties for our coop's newest member."

His edginess returning, Rick looked up. "Oh yeah, like what, Dirk?" he asked rudely.

"Like picking up where Craig left off, licking the stalls clean," he laughed. "Or, perhaps you'd rather me take you back to finish your little swim?"

Rick clammed up and shook his head. There was no way he wanted to relive his experience in the water trough.

Not a chance. For once he allowed common sense to prevail and kept his beak shut.

"And that's Mr. Stevens to you!" Dirk added with a smile, reinforcing his return to power. "I'm in charge now, and from here on in you will address me appropriately."

"Now get going!" he barked at all the fowl, who responded by doing just that.

Thirteen

It took a little over an hour to complete the duties as Mr. Stevens had instructed. The hens quickly returned to the henhouse and diligently tidied up; repairing broken nests, sweeping out stalls and wiping up egg yolk. One by one the hurtful messages were taken down off the Face-Beak walls and were discarded on the garbage heap along with the broken eggshells and stray feathers that had been strewn about during the riots. Once the henhouse was back to its normal state, each hen quietly returned to her own stall to pinch out some eggs. It was time to get back to work and keep the farmer happy. Playtime had officially ended.

Amidst all the grunting and groaning, Gladys took a moment for personal reflection. *What an idiot I have been. Losing my best friend over a stupid rooster.* The more Gladys reflected, the sadder she became. How short sighted she had been.

At the other end of the henhouse, Janet was experiencing similar feelings of regret. Rick, as it turned out, had been nothing more than a dirty, lying, reprobate. To steal his affection she had betrayed the trust of her BFF. Janet now hated herself for it. Blinded with lust, she had resorted to hiding behind Face-Beak to publicly humiliate Gladys. Although the posts were now long gone, the damage could never be undone. Sorrow washed over her, as a river of tears flowed down her face.

While the rest of the brood continued cleaning their stalls and filling their nests with eggs, the sobs of the two former BFFs could be heard echoing throughout the henhouse; a harsh reminder of the poor choices they had made.

Over in the Rooster Club, the boys spent the better part of an hour throwing away betting slips and dismantling their fighting octagon. Darryl, Dwayne and Marty were released from the lock-up and all three sheepishly worked alongside their fellow roosters restoring order to their home. Rick had disappeared to his stall, too embarrassed to show his beak. Not one of the roosters complained. As far as they were concerned, Rick was a piece of grit; a degenerate who had almost destroyed the harmony and happiness of their coop. The longer he spent out of sight, the better it was for all involved.

A package of cigarettes lay out on one of the tables. Darryl carefully picked it up and carried it over to the garbage heap. "What in the name of Mother-Cluck were we thinking?" he chirped to Dwayne, dropping the forbidden sticks onto the pile. "How did we ever let things get so out of hand?"

Dwayne lowered his head and shook it slowly in shame. There were no words to describe how disgusted and disappointed he was with himself. He had acted like a total greaseball. Out of the corner of his eye he caught a glimpse of Derek, his former bestie, sweeping his stall and chomping on a fresh bag of salt 'n' vinegar chips. *Would he ever forgive them for the horrible way he had been treated?*

*   *   *

By the imposed deadline, the chickens all reported back to the perch. Even Rick returned with the group, prepared to face the music. Mr. Stevens stood; keel out, once again the undisputed leader of the coop. He was angry, but effectively held his emotions in check as he addressed his fellow fowl.

"I think we need to reflect on the events that have transpired in the barnyard over the last couple of days," he clucked. "In order to be successful moving forward we must first confront our past." The chickens nodded in agreement. They had been total idiots, and it was time to own up to that fact.

"All of you need to give your combs a real good shake," Mr. Stevens began. "Your conduct over the last twenty four hours has been nothing short of disgraceful."

"Janet and Gladys," he chirped angrily, singling out the two female ringleaders. "You two have been friends forever. You were born in adjacent nests on the same day for crying out loud. The fact that you resorted to posting personal secrets about one another on Face-Beak sickens me. Makes me want to puke. It has shown us all what a couple of gutless cowards the two of you truly are. How is it possible to build trust in one another when at the drop of a hat you resort to public shaming to resolve your differences? As BFFs you didn't even have the decency to talk to one another face to face. Because of that, every chicken, donkey, sheep and cow, on this farm knows that Gladys has rooster parts, and that Janet has an unidentified fungus growing under her wings. Unbelievable!"

"No matter what happens between the two of you from here on in, your trust in each other will never be the same. Whether you resolve your issues or not, your friendship, as it was, is over." Gladys and Janet began sobbing uncontrollably as Mr. Stevens continued dressing them down.

"Face-Beak was created as a communication tool, not so you could publicly bully and harass one another. When used properly, it can be a very effective way of passing along information. When abused, it becomes nothing more than a forum for the cowardly and weak. A weapon! Those who use it have an obligation to do so responsibly. At this, you have failed miserably." He stared at both Janet and Gladys, neither of whom would make eye contact with him. They were too ashamed of their behaviour to look at anything other than the ground.

"The rest of you pullets are just as bad," he squawked angrily, taking a shot at the other hens. "Rather than coming to your friends' aid to help them resolve the situation, you stepped in and stirred the pot. You wedged yourselves into a situation that was none of your business and escalated it to the point where these two besties were ready to kill one other. At least Gladys and Janet had something to argue over, kinda. Do the rest of you even know what you were fighting about?"

A set of stunned, blank faces stared back at Mr. Stevens causing him, once again, to shake his head in disgust. "I didn't think so." Pointing a wing at the hens, he finished with an angry, "Shame on you all!" The hens sniffled and chirped apologies to one another. Most were in tears, overcome with remorse.

Convinced his message had gotten through to the ladies, Mr. Stevens turned his focus to the roosters. "You meatheads!" he exclaimed in exasperation, "all deserve a good kick in the giblets for your asinine behaviour. Smoking? Cockfighting? What were you thinking? Acting like a bunch of savages to impress," he nodded towards Rick, "this unit?"

"My brother Derek lost his two best friends, over what? A package of cigarettes and a ridiculous looking tattoo?" Glaring at his brother's former best friends, daring them to answer, "Darryl and Dwayne, you cast Derek aside like yesterday's trash so you could take up a stinky habit and hang out with a moron. You tossed away a lifelong friendship without even a second thought. My brother, who would give you his last bag of chips if you needed it, has been crushed. Crushed because you cared more about impressing Rick than you did for someone who has always been a good friend to you."

Darryl and Dwayne glanced over at Derek who quickly turned away, avoiding eye contact. Shaking a wing in a scolding gesture, Mr. Stevens continued lambasting the roosters. "Here's a newsflash for all of you. Being cool doesn't mean putting others down. And being cool certainly shouldn't involve forgetting who you really are. If you have to change your whole identity to impress another fowl, then maybe that fowl isn't worth impressing." The roosters looked around at one another sheepishly, ashamed by their ridiculous antics.

Mr. Stevens concluded his lecture by singling out the catalyst that had started it all. "Finally, there's you, Rick. You came waltzing in here under false pretenses with full intentions of turning this coop upside down. Your womanizing threw the henhouse in a tizzy and your smoking, and cockfighting nearly destroyed the rooster population."

"Rick, most of us would like nothing more than to ship you back to Farmer Beaton's. You are a troublemaker and an all around pain in the saddle. But we, unlike you, believe in showing mercy. So here it is . . ." The chickens all waited with bated breath.

"In order to remain in this coop, living with us, you are going to have to agree to abide by our former rules, in addition to following a few special, non-negotiable conditions," Mr. Stevens explained. "Think of it as our own little peace treaty. You *must* agree to *all* the demands or it's back to Farmer Beaton's for you."

"Sounds like I don't have much choice in the matter, do I?" Rick chirped, shrugging his wings.

"Nope," Mr. Stevens replied, with a smug little chirp of his own.

"Well, lay it out for me then," Rick sighed in defeat.

"Gladly," he replied, a smile forming on his beak. "For starters, you will agree that this little episode of mass chaos, anarchy and atrocious behaviour has been your fault."

"Whatever," Rick scoffed. "It's *all* my fault," he retorted with little sincerity. "Are we done yet?"

"Not even close amigo, not by a long shot," Mr. Stevens answered as he continued to outline the guidelines of the new pact. "The second condition involves you helping both the roosters and hens fix all remaining damages that were caused as a result of your flawed leadership. Riots, cockfights, they're all on you. You set them up, you can help clean them up." A scowl formed on Rick's beak. He hated work of any sort.

"Three. You will repay *all* the kibble you took as a result of the illegal cockfighting operation."

This point raised serious ire in Rick's psyche. "That's not fair," he argued. "I earned that kibble fair and square."

Shrugging, and laughing at Rick's complaints, Mr. Stevens delivered the final blow, "And last but not least, condition number four; you will promise to never, ever, build up forces, form alliances, or band together with others to overthrow the leadership of this coop again."

Rick shook his head in defeat. "So basically, you're saying I can't have any fun," he summarized in a tone laced with distaste.

"Basically," Mr. Stevens agreed with a nod.

Rick dipped his head with the enthusiasm of a sleeping warthog. There was nothing he could do. Throwing his wings up in defeat, he begrudgingly agreed to the terms. Reaching under his wing he pulled out a cigarette. "I really need a smoke after listening to all this crap."

"Ah, I almost forgot. Seeing as we have reverted back to our original rules and regulations, the smoking ban is back in effect," Mr. Stevens said, reaching up and grabbing the cigarette from Rick's beak. "No more smoking. This is, and will always be, a non-smoking coop,"

"But, that's not fair," Rick complained. "I like to smoke."

"And the rest of us like fresh air. There will be no smoking. Not in my coop!" clucked Mr. Stevens.

"Argh!" Rick squawked to no one in particular. "This place is like a prison."

"Yes, just like a prison," Mr. Stevens agreed. "Now maybe you should get started with your work. We've already wasted enough time bickering. Perhaps you can begin by helping Craig out a little. He needs some cool mud for his wattles, to help reduce the swelling."

Rick stood and glowered back at Mr. Stevens, "This is a load of bull . . ."

"Perhaps Farmer Beaton's would provide an environment of greater equality?" Mr. Stevens interrupted mid-sentence.

"Oh for the love of Mother-Cluck!" Rick squawked in defeat. "Where do I find the mud?

Fourteen

As the sun began to set, things were more or less back to normal in the coop. Nests were full of eggs and the hens had taken the first few steps toward living in harmony once again. Janet and Gladys apologized to one another and agreed to try and build back some of the trust that had been lost during their bitter dispute. Deep down though, both realized their friendship would never be the same.

Darryl, Dwayne and Derek also worked towards making amends, albeit begrudgingly. Derek was still hurting deeply from the shunning he had received at the wings of his two best friends. But, he would slowly get over it as time passed. Both Dwayne and Darryl were being extra nice to him, bringing in a seemingly endless supply of salt 'n' vinegar chips. Thus Derek decided he'd milk their generosity for all it was worth, one chomp at a time.

Mr. Stevens was back as master of his domain, much to everyone's relief. He had restored order in the coop, and saved his fellow fowl, once again, from a sure disaster. Standing at the fence, staring out at the pasture on the west side of the farm, he settled in to enjoy the sunset.

"Hey handsome," a voice called out from behind. Mr. Stevens turned to see Sandra approaching. "Join me for a cigarette?"

"Very funny," Mr. Stevens replied with a chuckle. "How about joining me for the sunset instead?"

"I guess," she replied grabbing hold of his wing and holding it in hers.

"How are things in the henhouse?"

"Getting there," she replied with a smile. "No more drama. No more cliques. A whole lot of tears and remorse. Rooster Club?"

Mr. Stevens shook his head. "No more smoking and no more fighting. *And*, a whole lot of sucking up to my brother Derek. All in all, I'd say things are straightening themselves out."

Both stood quietly for a moment, enjoying the brilliant colours that filled the evening sky. "You were great today Dirk," Sandra praised. "Once again, you saved this coop from certain disaster." Mr. Stevens smiled. He couldn't imagine anything nicer than standing, enjoying the sunset, with the beautiful Sandra Thompson. He looked into her deep blue eyes, and she returned his loving gaze. Mr. Stevens, sensing the moment had arrived, leaned in to rub beaks with the hen of his dreams . . .

"Hey there love birds!" A voice cried out from behind, breaking the calm of the twilight. "Hope I'm not interrupting anything." The two wheeled around to find Derek, standing behind them, munching on a fresh bag of kettle boiled chips.

"Great timing bro," Mr. Stevens muttered under his breath.

Sandra laughed. "It's good to see you smiling again Derek. And enjoying your favourite snack." Turning to Mr. Stevens she smiled and let go of his wing. "It's been a long day, so I think I'm going to head back and hit the nest. But, I'll see you two boys in the morning. Bright and early!" Gingerly, she leaned over and gave Mr. Stevens a peck on the cheek. "Goodnight Dirk."

Mr. Stevens watched as she waddled off towards the henhouse.

The two brothers stood silently, the chomping of fresh, kettle-cooked chips being the only sound. Hesitantly, Derek held the open bag out to Mr. Stevens. "Here bro, have a chip," he offered.

Surprised, Mr. Stevens reached into the bag and helped himself to a wingful. "Thanks," he replied. It was the first time on record that Derek had ever shared his sacred snack with any-fowl.

"Figured sharing my chips was the least I could do to thank you for helping me get my two best friends back," Derek replied, slowly breaking eye contact and staring at the ground. "Given our past history, you would have had every right to ignore my pleas for assistance."

Mr. Stevens flashed a grin at his brother. "Well to be honest with you Derek, it was actually kind of nice being on the same side for once," he replied truthfully. "Maybe while the rest of the brood is settling their issues, we can do the same with ours."

Derek nodded in agreement. "I think that's your best idea yet."

Mr. Stevens reached over and gave his brother a big hug. "Tell you what big bro, tomorrow morning, why don't you come out and give the morning wake up call with me."

Derek stared back at him in shock. The morning wake up call was the highest honour a rooster could receive. "R-R-Really," he stammered. "Are you serious?"

"Ya, I'm serious," Mr. Stevens replied. "You had the decency to share your chips with me, so, sharing my perch is the least *I* can do."

Derek laughed. "Sounds good."

"I guess that means we better hit the hay ourselves," Mr. Stevens suggested. "Six o'clock will be here in no time and we have to be ready." Laughing and joking the two brothers headed back to the Rooster Club.

"Should I do the call with or without chips in my beak?" Derek wondered out loud.

Mr. Stevens shrugged, "Whatever feels natural bro. It's totally up to you."

As the two retired for the night, they did so knowing that things were back to normal in the coop. On the edge of catastrophe and the cusp of disaster, Dirk Stevens had once again restored order to Farmer Johnston's barnyard.

Epilogue

"I told you Myrtle, we're gonna have to do something about these dang hens," Farmer Johnston complained as he and his wife descended upon the coop. The market had been a total disaster and the farmer was ready to exact a little revenge. He'd eaten nothing but bunt cakes all afternoon and was a little bit testy as bedtime approached. Slowly he removed his belt from the loops of his jeans. "It's time I teach these dumb birds a lesson," he threatened, slapping his hand with the leather strap.

"Relax Jim," Myrtle Johnston replied. "Let's see what we've got here before you start smacking the birds around."

"I'll tell you what we got here Myrtle. We got a mess on our hands, and no eggs. These stupid cluckers are going to learn a little bit about work ethic tonight with a little visit from Mr. Leather," he replied, referring to his belt.

As the two entered the henhouse they were met by a shocking sight. Every nest was overloaded with eggs.

"What the . . ." Farmer Johnston began before his wife chimed in.

"Look at all these eggs," she affirmed, staring at her husband, confused. "These nests are all jammed full. I thought you told me they were empty."

The farmer looked at his wife, "They *were* empty. I swear on the good name of old Mother-Cluck they were. When I came in here this morning there wasn't an egg to be found."

Myrtle gently placed her arm around her husband's shoulder. "It's okay Jim," she said softly. "I think we should hold off on having those enchiladas for a little while. Maybe you got yourself a little dehydrated and disoriented with all that uh, sickness you had last night."

"No. No way. These nests were empty this morning. I wasn't dehydrated, and I wasn't disoriented. These nests were empty! These little cluckers must've been laying eggs all afternoon."

"Right," Myrtle replied sarcastically, rolling her eyes. "Empty at six thirty and then full with the equivalent of about seven days worth of eggs by nightfall. Believable tale Jim!"

From her nest, Sandra Thompson could hear the farmer and his wife arguing. She couldn't help but chuckle as the dumbfounded farmer tried to convince his wife that he wasn't crazy. Once again, things had returned to normal. The henhouse high jinx was finally over.

The End

One

The sun rose over the east corner of the henhouse. Mr. Thompson slowly strutted out to his perch on the fencepost. The morning sun glistened off his muscular body, and his shiny feathers gleamed, as he reared back his handsome head, stretched out his mighty wings and bellowed, "Cockle-doodle-doo!" The alarm clock had sounded. It was time for all the snoozing barnyard animals to wake up and begin their busy day.

The chickens all stared with open-beaked awe. As far as roosters were concerned, Mr. Thompson was 'The Giblets'. Every single young cockerel in Farmer Johnston's chicken coop was envious of Mr. Thompson, from the tips of his strapping comb to the bottoms of his brawny feet. Mr. Thompson was the biggest, bravest, most striking rooster in the entire brood. With his carefully groomed tail feathers, honeyed keel and immaculately maintained coiffure, Mr. Thompson was what all considered to be, 'high-society fowl'.

Little Dirk Stevens was especially impressed by the mighty Mr. Thompson and would often mimic him when the other fowl weren't looking. "I sure do hope that one day I can be the rooster who gives the morning wake up call," he clucked to no one in particular. Dirk's lout of an older brother, Derek, overheard the comment and erupted in wing slapping hysteria.

"You?" he replied with a jiggling belly, "giving the wake-up call? Only the strongest, most handsome rooster has that honour. A useless wimp like you will never be up on Mr. Thompson's perch. Little sissies like you amount to nothing more than table fodder. Little sissies like you would never be called mister," Derek cackled.

Dirk held his head in shame. It was true. He was a gigantic wuss; slow, weak, and unable to stand up for himself. It wasn't really his fault. He had been the egg at the edge of the nest that hadn't received enough warmth and attention. While other chickens were developing normally in their pre-hatched state, Dirk was little more than a shivering yolk. At least that's what Derek always said. As a result, Dirk Stevens was a little smaller and a lot slower than the other chickens.

"Stop tormenting your brother," Dirk's mother piped up. "Your brother isn't useless, he's good for lots of things."

"Oh yeah maw," Derek shot back, "name one use he has, other than being an appetizer."

Mother Stevens thought for a moment, made a motion like she was about to speak, paused for another second, then waddled off. "I think I hear someone calling my name, I'll get back to you on that one."

The shame continued to build in poor Dirk. Even his own mother couldn't find a single good thing to say about him. His own mother! This set his brother off in yet another wave of wattle shaking hysterics.

"Haw, haw. Even mom thinks you are a loser," Derek scoffed. "That's pathetic."

At least I'm not a gluttonous, overweight, root beer guzzling, chip eating, foul smelling degenerate, thought Dirk to himself. To the common observer Derek Stevens truly was a standout, and not in the positive sense of the word. He was a big rooster. Big rooster. Not big as in muscular, but big as in grossly obese. A glandular condition coupled with an acute addiction to salt and vinegar potato chips led to the development of his less than svelte figure. Derek was rarely seen without a bag of goodies tucked under his wing. His day was never complete unless he took a few pot shots at his younger, weaker sibling.

Dirk never chirped back at his brother. He'd learned that lesson the hard way. In anger one day, he mentioned something about Derek's breath, comparing it to the smell of the rotting delights in Farmer Johnston's compost pile. Derek, less than pleased, had responded quickly and efficiently by sitting on his brother, full weight, for three hours. During the event Derek had breathed heavily in his brother's face. The stench alone made Dirk reconsider ever talking back again. He had since kept his beak shut and begrudgingly accepted his brother's constant badgering.

As if having his brother riding his saddle wasn't bad enough, back-up soon arrived. Dwayne and Darryl, Derek's two best friends, came waddling up. They were clucking and chirping back and forth like a couple of meat birds. Dwayne and Darryl, much like Dirk's brother Derek, lacked a little in the brain department. A fact that became more and more apparent each time they opened their beaks. They too enjoyed tormenting Dirk. Abusing Dirk, however, was not the first thing on Dwayne and Darryl's agenda.

"Derek," Dwayne chirped. "Have you seen Sandra today? She looks smoking hot!" Darryl stood next to his friend and nodded his head up and down so hard his wattles shook.

"Oh man," Derek squawked. "Her tail feathers were looking mighty fine yesterday."

"Well, they are even better today, guaranteed. I think she spent a little extra time preening in the stall this morning. I saw her and nearly passed out from her radiance, true story." Darryl blurted out through a barrage of heavy breathing.

"I could stare at her saddle all day long," Dwayne added. The three all nodded in unison staring off into another world.

"What I wouldn't give to rub beaks with her out behind the barn," Derek fantasized, drooling like a three-month old baby.

Dirk was appalled by the roosters' lewd discussion. Sandra Thompson was indeed a fine looking hen. She was also the eldest daughter of Mr. Thompson and a proper young lady at that. She was a highly educated and moral young pullet who certainly should be spoken about in much higher regard. Dirk felt that the filthy talk of his brother and friends, however true, was very inappropriate. Rather than keeping his thoughts to himself he decided to open his beak and chirp his mind.

"You shouldn't be speaking so disrespectfully about Sandra," he said, scolding Derek, Dwayne and Darryl. "Your level of rudeness is totally unacceptable."

The three roosters looked at Dirk and tilted their heads. They glared at him with a look of disdain. Derek turned and nodded at Dwayne, Dwayne nodded at Darryl, and Darryl nodded at Derek. Dirk began to feel a little nervous when he realized no one was nodding at him.

"Gee Dirk, maybe you're right." Dwayne said slowly. "Maybe we are being disrespectful." His words dripped with sarcasm. The three began to slowly approach.

"I don't know," disagreed Darryl. "I think we were being very complimentary with our comments." The others nodded in agreement.

"Very complimentary," Derek agreed. He took a moment and pretended to think.

"Maybe Dirk needs to learn what disrespect truly looks like," Derek proposed. "Perhaps a barnyard breath freshener will help him understand disrespect a little better." All three nodded again then snickered in unison.

Dirk cowered in fear. The barnyard breath freshener, or BBF for short, was the most repugnant punishment a rooster could receive; so vile and disgusting it can't even be described. Dirk had woken up with the sweats many times after nightmares of being on the receiving end of a BBF. His nightmares, it seemed, were finally coming to fruition.

The three swooped down on the weakling and pushed him to the ground. Luckily for Dirk, Farmer Johnston chose that very moment to come out to the trough with the daily feed. The daily feed trumped all other activities, regardless of their importance, thus Dirk was momentarily saved from the humiliation of the dreaded BBF.

All the chickens in the coop swarmed quickly as scrumptious mealworm and freshly harvested corn niblets were spread in the dirt. Dirk cast aside his problems for the moment and quickly waddled over to join the feeding frenzy. There was nothing like a full belly, followed by a nap to make one's troubles disappear.

As usual, Dirk was too small and too weak to battle to the front of the raucous crowd. When he finally reached the spot that moments earlier had been bountiful with nourishment, there was only one single, wilted kernel of corn left. In spite of the meagre helping, Dirk's beak still watered with anticipation at the thought of having his daily meal. Just as he was about to snap up his find, he found himself being violently shoved to the ground.

"I'll take that!" declared Derek as he snapped up the last morsel. "Yummy! That was some good eating."

"Hey!" Dirk shouted. "That was mine. I didn't get anything to eat. You stole it from me"

"Eat some dirt bro," Derek laughed. "Or chow down on some bugs. Not like a little food is going to make you any tougher."

Dwayne and Darryl returned to throw a few jabs of their own at little Dirk as he slowly stood up and dusted himself off.

"You're such a runt, they wouldn't even serve you on Wing Night!" Darryl joked maliciously, giving Dirk a poke in the keel that knocked him back down to the ground.

"Is that a comb, or did your head just throw up?" Dwayne chimed in, pointing his wing cruelly at the crooked feature on the top of Dirk's melon.

"You just wait little brother," Derek chirped, "that mealworm is going to make me good and gassy. When it does we will be coming around to feed you your BBF. In fact I can feel my gizzards begin to gurgle already. You're lucky it's nap time or you'd be getting your due right now." The three broke into fits of laughter once again.

Dirk angrily stood up and shook himself off, "Someday you, and all the other chickens in this coop, are going to wish you had been nicer to me." The guffaws only grew louder as Dirk waddled back to his stall.

Acknowledgements

Rob and Eric would like to extend a big Cockle-Doodle-Doo to the following wonderful people for their support of this project:

Anne Davies for being that editing force; reading through countless versions of the script when she literally has a thousand other things to do.

Shawn Beaton has been one of Mr. Stevens best buds from the very beginning, offering suggestions and critiques as well as his own editing expertise.

Glen Earley, a fantastic teaching partner who continues to fuel the fire and weigh in on plot-lines and characters. Glen can take full credit for the invention of Face-Beak-It's his!

Alex Surrett of Surreal Marketing for his social media expertise, and his creation of the ePub versions available on Amazon and iTunes.

Special thanks to Earl Thomas and Evan Villadores at Trafford Publishing for handling our many needs as we moved forward to print. It's been great working with such dedicated professionals.

Last but not least, to our friends and families who put up with us every day! Thanks for all the love and support!